Sundays in the Dojo

Sundays in the Dojo

The Making of a Warrior-Priest

Don S. Lewis Ph.D.

22nd Century Institute, LLC
Stanardsville, VA
www.22ci.org

Cover Design: Benjamin J. Lewis, bicyclebutter@gmail.com

Photo: Shay White, shaywhitephotography.com

ISBN-10: 0983259801

ISBN: 978-0-9832598-0-0

First printing 2011

ATTENTION CORPORATIONS, UNIVERSITIES, COLLEGES AND PROFESSIONAL ORGANIZATIONS.

Quantity discounts are available purchases of this book for educational, gift purposes, or as premiums for increasing magazine subscriptions or renewals. Special books or book excerpts can also be created to fit specific needs. For information, please contact: 22nd Century Institute, PO Box 356, Stanardsville, VA 22973; ph. 434-985-8737.

Dedicated to

Jane: my wife, lover, best friend, co-philosopher and co-theologian, and fellow Warrior-Priest,

And to our children, Ben and Cara, who have made our lives complete, full, and exciting.

Sundays In The Dojo:

The Making of a Warrior-Priest

A Personal Note from the Author

Within these pages are story and myth, not history. The events, as told, are not real. The characters are imaginary.

While told in the context of martial arts, this is not just a story of martial arts. Rather, it is a metaphor for all of life. It teaches the lessons of finding one's personal power by facing both the good and the bad side that each of us has within ourselves.

Likewise, being a Warrior does not necessarily mean doing so in the physical sense. There are many Warriors in the world who do not fight physical battles. Some are social workers, some attorneys, some teachers, some managers, some CEOs, and some visionaries.

Regardless of their calling, Warriors are those who stand on the boundary line between the victim and the oppressor. Warriors are willing to pay the price of losing their personal peace for the greater peace of the whole world.

The Dojo has never existed in the physical form described in this book. It actually started in a locker room. Since then it has existed in several different university gymnasiums, a university wrestling room, an unused pump house on an old estate, a commercial dining room after hours, an aerobics room at a health club, a garage, and under an open-air carport, to name a few incarnations.

The events are all based on some incident that occurred to one of us: a student, a client, or friends. The events are faithful to the emotional impact on the individuals who lived them. They are not historical renderings of what actually happened. They are founded in the coherence theory of truth rather than the correspondence theory.

The story is allegory and mythology. The emotional struggles of Les were some of the struggles that I went through as well as an amalgamation of issues from students and clients we have had across the years. Basically the idea for the story and many of the lessons learned came from my struggles with who I am and the difficulty I had finding an acceptance of the two sides of myself.

MOST IMPORTANTLY OF ALL: I gave Les two mentors, Don and Jane. I used our own names because this book is intended to be a dialogue between the reader and ourselves. Don and Jane, as I portrayed us in the book, are highly idealized versions of who we really are; anyone who has studied under us and reads this book will know that immediately. They will find the portrayals of us amusing at a minimum and, toward the other end of the spectrum, a tall tale. Most likely, they will break into gales of laughter and shake their heads, wondering if I've lost touch with reality. I haven't.

I know who we are and how different that is from the version portrayed here. This is story. It is designed to be allegory and mythology, and everything is larger than life. The characters of Don and Jane are there to teach principles and concepts through their words and actions. They are an accurate portrayal of our thoughts and beliefs, but not necessarily of how we interact, talk, or live out our lives.

If you read this book and should happen to study with us sometime in the future, you will find yourself very disappointed if you don't understand the phrase "highly idealized". If you don't get that concept yet, read it over and over until you do. Underline the words "highly idealized".

I decided to write the characters of Don and Jane this way because the book is really about two versions of myself. Don and Jane as written, represent the middle-aged version of ourselves mentoring the younger version of myself in a way that I wish someone could have done for me. They also represent the mythological version of what I wished I had had as instructors.

I had several wonderful mentors during my growing-up and young adult years to whom I am very grateful. But none of them were able to take me through this part of my journey; I found Warriors or Priests but not Warrior-Priests, at least in the realm of physical battles. I found no one to lead me on this part of my journey at that time. Simply put, this is me now, telling the person I was then that it was going to be okay.

Since I have gotten older and worked through these struggles, I have found other Warrior-Priests. Sadly, there were none there for me when I needed them. In this book I created them for Les. I hope that this book will also serve as a surrogate mentor for those readers who have such a need.

I am eternally grateful to my wife Jane, who has been on this journey with me. She is not just my lover, my wife, the mother of my children, and my best friend, but she is also my co-philosopher and co-theologian. It was through our dialogues, debates, and sometimes, out-and-out arguments over issues that this philosophy, and thus, Waboku Jujitsu has come to be. Without her this system would not exist. Without her I would not have found peace within myself.

Waboku Jujitsu is a growing and living system. It has seen several incarnations including one major revision. It is more about philosophy and personal growth than technique. While the techniques are good and work well, if the person doesn't grow in the learning of the system, then it has been a pointless exercise. The techniques are first and foremost tools to help people become all they were created to be. The role of an instructor in our system is to help the students become all that they can be through the learning of the techniques.

One last comment: We both work from a Christian perspective, but don't let the metaphors confuse you or get you upset. If you come out of a Muslim background, then replace God with Allah. If you are Jewish, choose Yahweh or one of many other names. If you are New Age, choose "the Universe" to replace God. Choose whatever metaphor works for you; we really don't care. Just find peace for yourself in a way that improves the quality of the world, not one that lessens it. There is enough tragedy in this world through natural occurrences without having to add to it by fighting over whose metaphor is right.

I hope that the reading of these pages will bring on Sabbath moments: times that are sacred and apart, comforting and troubling. We pray that it is the Sabbath for you whenever you pick up this book. Enter into the Dojo through these pages to wrestle with life and God, to grow, to argue, to wonder at the universe, and to become. Enter into this journey and continue or begin to walk, balanced on the edge of the sword.

This work of fiction provides lessons on finding the path to your own personal power. Along with two other books it makes up the *What to Do While Waiting for Peace to Come* triology. *The Warrior's Codex: Sayings from the Heart of a Warrior* teaches these lessons through sayings and proverbs. *Developing Warriors for the 22nd Century: What to Do While Waiting for Peace to Come,* teaches the same lessons through a non-fiction explanatory text.

New Year's Day, 2008

Dear Ted,

Just as you and your family were packing to leave this Christmas, you caught me off to one side of the car and raised a number of questions. I wish we had had time to sit and talk them over, but often the most important questions are asked at the moment of leaving—probably because the questioner needs to have an exit plan.

We all tend to do that. We raise the questions and then we leave. We hope that somehow the distance between the one who answers and ourselves will reduce both the panic we feel and the fear that haunts us about what the answers may be.

So let's see how I do at remembering them. If I leave any out or if others arise, just let me know.

Is it true that you and grandma met at the Dojo?
Did you really have to kill some people in a fight?
How? What did it feel like? Was it easy? Who were they?
Why didn't you train my mom in martial arts?
Could I come and live with you and Grandma and have you train me?
Would I be any good? I'm not that good at sports.
Mom said that she named me after a great warrior who was one of our ancestors, but she can't remember who he was. Is that true? (I assume that by 'Is that true?' you mean. 'Did she name you after a great warrior?' as we all know that she would do the forgetting part.)

What of Helena? Wasn't she named after a warrior too? And why did Mom pick warriors?

And your last two questions, Ted, came after I told you in response that you were a Warrior and soon it would be time to start your training. You asked, "You mean I should join the army? And how do you know that I am a Warrior?"

So let me answer the last ones first, as they are the easiest.

Do I mean that you should join the army?
    No. Not for some time to come. After that it will be your choice, but joining or not joining has nothing to do with being a Warrior.

How do I know that you are a Warrior? (Note that I am using a capital W.)
    There are lots of ways of knowing, just as there are lots of ways of seeing or hearing. For now let's just say that your grandmother and I know. We agree. You are a Warrior and the time for your training is at hand.

Is Helena a Warrior too?
    Yes, but her time for training has not come. After all, she is three years younger than you and only thirteen. She needs some time.

Were you and Helena both named after great warriors who were our ancestors?
    Well, yes and no. You were both named after the same warrior who lived in the last half of the nineteenth century and died in the early twentieth century. She was not of our bloodline, but of our spiritual family. There are lots of ways to be family. Who she is and how she relates to us we will reveal to you in time.

And how like your mother to get the general idea and forget the details! While they are twins, your mother and your aunt are almost total opposites. Your aunt's the lawyer and your mom's the poet. Your mom knows the broad sweep of the meaning of the

Dojo, but the details … Maybe that was why she stopped learning after Green Belt. But make no mistake. She can fight and fight well.

Can you live with us and train with us?

We would need to discuss that with your parents. At this point Grandma and I think it might be better for you to stay with your family and finish high school. During that time you could train with us whenever you can until you graduate. (I know, I know … Damn all adults and their strange sense of responsibility!)

There are two colleges around here so maybe after you graduate from high school you could come to one of them. In less than two years you could begin the serious work you will need to learn here at the Dojo. You will be good. We can see that, even if you can't. But if you truly cannot wait, begin by talking with them. If they find themselves feeling that it may be important, then we will all talk.

Ted, we watched you struggle while you were here. Across your vacation time here at Christmas, we saw—and recognized—some of the struggles you are going through. Your mom and dad have seen it as normal teenage angst. We know that it is more. You are struggling with your calling.

It goes back many years. When you first went with us as a toddler many years ago, the way that you walked into the Dojo with us was telling. You, who always ran loudly through everything, came in, stopped in your place, plunked down on your diapered bottom, and just looked around. The way you entered it this time with your awe, your fear, and now your questions, was even more indicative.

And across the years, your numerous trips to the Dojo when you thought no one was looking … You thought no one had noticed those late nights when you snuck over to the Dojo and sat there quietly in the dark, sometimes for several hours. And your walks in the woods. They all said to us that something is driving you toward a good discontentment on the inside.

There is a Greek term, *kairos*. It means "when the time is right," as opposed to *chronos*, which is clock or calendar time. We think that it is kairos for you to find out not only the answers to some of the questions you asked, but it is also time for you to know even more than you could know to ask.

I have been meaning to write some of this down for several years, but now it seems that kairos has come for both of us. I have purchased a "speak and write" program for the computer and am experimenting with it. Within a week or so I will commit to talk (write) for an hour or so a day. I will speak my story as it relates to the Dojo and my wife of so many years. I will send you one or two chapters at a time as I finish them. I will eventually put them into a book and they would need to be edited for that, but you get the raw version with only spell check and cursory grammar check. That will begin to answer some of the rest of the questions that you have asked.

We love you so much and we want the very best for you. If the struggle seems really hard at night, go somewhere quiet—somewhere sacred to you—center yourself, and then call out to us in silence. We will respond. Where is the sacred place for you? And what do I mean by that? And what do I mean by "center yourself"? You will find those answers yourself when you are ready. That's kairos and that's how it works.

Love,

Grandpa Les

one

The Ceremony

Only six years older than you are now, your grandmother sat motionless before our instructors, kneeling on the mats while I moved slowly toward a bench on the back wall. Careful to not make a sound or any sudden moves, I had one hand on the wall to the right of the door, trying to steady myself. I hated to return to the Dojo like this (yes, the same Dojo as the one by our house) and I hated myself for it. After four months of avoiding this place I had been forced to return.

I had wanted to return, and had tried several times. But I just hadn't been able to make myself come back. I should have handled it like falling off of a horse: you get back up and right back on. But I hadn't. And each week it became more and more of an impossible task. But because of her I was here now. And only because I had promised.

We had a big fight over my not coming to her Black Belt test, but the thought of returning to the Dojo would bring a wave of nausea anytime it entered my mind. As soon as I would give up the idea of returning, I would start to get better … That's not true; I wouldn't *get* better—I would just *feel* better. Still, to end the fight I had agreed to try to be there.

But I missed it. I was too sick to go that morning. I stayed in bed. She was hurt, but I guess seeing me with chills and fever and my missing two days of work convinced her I really had been sick. Or at least it kept her from killing me.

But missing this would not have been understood; she had made that very clear. It was her ceremony, her family was here, and I was to meet them. I remember her black eyes flashing; she had ended the argument by hurling the statement across the room, "That is the end of the

1

discussion or the end of us!" She punctuated it with a slamming door as she stomped out.

I didn't drive up with anyone. Leroy had offered to drive up with me, but I just didn't take him up on it. It would have brought back too many memories. So I came up alone. And late. I parked at the far end of the lane, and after making sure no one was on the road, I moved up until I got close to the clearing.

I stayed out of sight inside the tree line until the last few students hanging around outside looked up almost as one, as the soft sound of a ringing bowl drifted through the doors. They turned and went in. It was about to start.

Heart pounding and starting to sweat in spite of the chill, I started toward the doors, moving only because of my fear of losing Jenna. I knew that she loved me, but I don't know if she could have forgiven me if I missed this. I knew that I wouldn't have forgiven myself.

Silence filled the inside as the ringing of the bowl faded away. I stopped at the side of the door and with a quick glance inside I saw the class sitting silently in meditation and knew I was at the point where my entrance would be least noticeable.

But the pausing to look in had been too much. My stomach suddenly heaved and I choked back a nasty combination of liquid and small curds. I gulped in cool air, trying to calm my stomach and keep from vomiting. After two or three seconds standing there I knew that I couldn't take this indecision anymore, so I lunged forward. I reached the open doors and stepped quietly through.

My whole body had broken into a sweat and my shirt was wet, reeking of the bitter smell of nervous perspiration. I made it to the bench, leaned on the wall, and carefully lowered myself down, still uncertain of my stomach's intention. I was to meet her parents (your great-grandparents), so it gave me an excuse to dress up. And I deliberately hadn't brought my *gi*, so they wouldn't expect me to sit with the class. I just sat and tried to stay calm.

Breathing slowly, eyes closed, the instructors knelt at the front facing the class. There was no perceptible change in them when I slipped in the door, but I sensed that something had alerted them to the fact that I had returned. Knowing Don and Jane, it would have been almost impossible for them not to notice my presence. They wouldn't miss the waterfall of emotions tumbling over the cliff of my instability.

I just sat there, alone on the bench, and then tears started to flow as the memories flooded in: weekly practices and of techniques done over and over. Then suddenly, that day four months ago burst back into my life. Every other memory was gone. The present was gone, the future was gone; all that was left was those few awful seconds.

I had relived them over and over during the past four months. Not just remembered them—experienced them afresh. Many times a day. At first the memories had overlapped, with the scene starting over again before the previous one could end.

Over the last two months, I had gotten to where I could go the better part of a day without thinking of that scene. And the vividness of the memories had started to fade, too.

But now I was here. And the memories were back—full force. And then I was back there on that street; feeling the fear that had lasted only a split second before suddenly shifting into a state of no emotion. And then that overwhelming rush of body memories, those memories of the feel of flesh on flesh that had burned into my soul.

I was there. Again. Living it second by second—the present, not the past. Hard contact and the sudden cracking that I feel and hear when the structures under the skin give way. The impacts, her screams from behind me, more movement, more contact—then nothing.

No one moving. My eyes see no movement, my ears confirm the silence. Silence broken for only a moment by one last, loud attempt to breathe from the one in front of me, and then more silence. Then shock hits me, my eyes scan the scene and take in that awful view of the silence of sound and motion. Disbelief, sudden nausea.

Leaning on a building I can't remember how I got to and puking onto the sidewalk until I am shaking and cold. Then a far-off scream and the closer words from my other side: "Oh, shit man! What the hell did you do to 'em?"

Voices, someone yelling to get to a phone and call the cops. Sirens, police, medics shaking their heads as they glanced at the cops, handcuffs, the stink of the back seat of a patrol car. Questions. More questions through a window cracked open. Questions in through the car door, now open.

Then more in a room, with an attorney someone had called. Papers signed, a ride with my friends, and then I was home. Alone. Except for a room full of memories slamming into my head and oozing from every pore of my body. And Jenna and Leroy. Still, I was alone.

And sitting there in the Dojo that day I was reliving it again. Over and over. With all my senses. *In* all my senses—worse than I had for months. I never should have come. It had been a mistake. I had to leave. I needed fresh air.

The unholy mixture from my stomach burned as it started back up my throat. *I don't think I can't keep it down this time. It's coming up.* With that thought racing in my mind, I put a hand on the wall and moved my feet under me, leaning toward the door. Tears pouring out of my eyes blinded me and I paused, blinking madly, trying to see my way out.

Then a whirring sound and I was pulled out of that present, that past, out of that mess, and into some other now. Something was coming into focus. I'm not on that street anymore. I'm here. And then I heard his voice softly, but very firmly saying,

"Breathe."

It was a command. I followed it without thinking. I followed the pattern he was laying out.

"Breathe deeply. Slowly.

"Breathe in.

"Hold it.

"Breathe out.

"Focus.

"Relax with each breath out.

"Breathe in and go deeper inside.

"Breathe out and relax.

"Turn loose.

"Let the universe breathe you."

And the tornado of feelings and physical revulsion coalesced into some kind of chaotic order, slowed down, lessened, and started moving inside. I felt my self, my consciousness going deep, deep inside, but to a peaceful center this time. Not that awful pit.

This calming was out of my control, but it felt so good that I surrendered to the words. I gave in to the gentle commands. And for the first time since that awful few seconds, I reached that point of calm that I used to feel. Before that day. I breathed slowly, in and out, and my soul moved back into the room, into my self. He had spoken and the words had worked their magic.

We normally meditate in silence, so I didn't know why he had addressed these words to me out loud. I guess that he must have known how much I had needed that structured breathing.

Then it became clearer: the sound hadn't come through my ears. There wasn't even a sound. Just silence and unison breathing. The words had formed inside. My ears had not picked up the sound of his voice because he hadn't spoken aloud.

The words had formed in my head! Don was speaking to me in my mind and I had relaxed gently into the soothing sound and support of his voice. I remembered how stunned I had been the first time this happened. How much I had learned in the fourteen months that I studied here. And how much I had missed in the last four.

And now, after abruptly leaving, I had come back. Back to the Dojo, back to my temple, and had found that sacred spot inside of me again. I relaxed and opened my eyes. He had too. He was looking deep into my soul and he was smiling. Smiling! God, how I needed someone who knew, to understand and to smile. He slowly moved his eyes away and focused on the girl on the mat.

I willed myself back to this reality and looked around. Things looked just as they did four months ago when I walked out that Sunday, unaware and unprepared for what was to happen. I breathed in slowly again and looked around.

To the left of the doors, sitting on the benches around the walls, were a number of people I didn't know. At the end of one bench was a middle-aged couple I recognized from pictures as Jenna's parents. Her father obviously had been studying me intently. There was something so intense in his look, and yet I detected nothing but support.

He looked away from me and back to the front and to the unfolding ceremony being played out. I was too weak to really worry what he was thinking. At least I wasn't running out and blowing lunch on my way.

On the other side of him, sitting in a folding chair, was an older lady who I guessed was her grandmother. Past her on another bench were two fifteen or sixteen-year-old boys sitting together, and I figured one was her brother, Hank, and the other one maybe a friend. Next to them were two girls, probably her sisters. One was seventeen and one twenty, if I remembered right.

Still fighting to keep stuff down and in my stomach, I turned, and as I looked back to the front, it hit me that Jenna hadn't seen me come in and didn't know that I was there. She had wanted me to be there so badly and I had promised. She and I had talked about my coming to the ceremony over and over. While she understood my issues, she needed me there. I knew that I belonged here. I wanted to be here for this; I really wanted to see her get this belt.

But there was no way now that I could tell her that I had come. I wanted her to relax and enjoy, knowing that I had kept my word. But now there was no way to let her know, so I just sat.

But I had been unsure of what coming would cost me. She had given her all to it, but coming back was more than I was ready to do. While I knew that I needed to for myself, I hadn't been able to. In the end, maybe the ceremony was the only thing that would have brought me here, no matter how badly I needed to come.

Now that I had passed the first hurdle of getting here, I began to focus outside of myself. Harriet, one of the thirty-some-odd students who were on the mat, was sitting in her usual position, sideways with one leg stuck awkwardly out and leaning against the wall. Apparently, Harriet's bad hip forced her to adjust positions, and as she did, she gave out a soft groan as a wave of pain hit her. She had suffered a crushed pelvis in an accident and it had never completely healed, so this was common for her—so common that none of us even noticed it anymore during meditation.

I shifted in response to her discomfort, swallowed back down some more of the regurge slightly wrong, and wound up choking. I half coughed, half choked two or three times into the silence, fearing that was still going to bring up the mess I had just forced down.

Two or three of the class in the back row looked around and nodded. God! I know my face was red. I just wanted to see this ceremony and escape, although that wasn't possible either. I just wanted to ... Shit! I was just a mess. Oh well. Jenna didn't flinch, but at least she probably knew that I was here.

I looked to where she was kneeling alone in front of the class. Her hair matched the color of her belt and she was wearing it down and flowing. She looked gorgeous. As strange as it may be for you to under-stand, Ted, your grandmother was a real looker. Stunning. Still is in my eyes. Normally, she wore her hair up in a bun for class, but this was the first time I saw her with it down while she was dressed in her gi. She was beautiful.

The two instructors looked around at all of us and then focused their attention on her.

I sat back and released the tension—well, a little of it at least. Taking a couple more deep breaths, I looked slowly around and became fully aware of the Dojo. The room had a pleasant odor. There was the smell of the outdoors.

They must have aired out the dojo since the class earlier this morning. After the class the air usually had a somewhat pungent smell, although I don't remember it ever being offensive, and it smelled different, some-how, than most of the gyms I had been in.

The sunlight was streaming in from the windows on the roof. The angled panes made different patterns on the floor and over the group. As I followed one line of shadows, I noticed Leroy for the first time. He was sitting in the first row along with several of the other upper belts. But of course, my focus came back to Jenna, and then Don spoke.

"Warriors stand on the boundary line. Sometimes metaphorically. Sometimes legally or politically. And sometimes they physically stand on the line between the victim and the oppressor. Whatever the battlefield, the Warriors know that this is not a game. It is for real – or they wouldn't be there. They simply move into the drama and take their place. They know that by stepping onto that line that they have committed to take the process to the furthest extreme required of them.

"When they stand on the boundary line physically, they know they must be ready to kill. They do not desire to kill, but they know that it may have to be done. That is how they start the battle. They start, knowing that they are being called upon to do battle once again. They start know-ing that they may kill or that they may be killed. And while they will use all of their skills, which are usually considerable, they cannot control the outcome. They can only be there and do what must be done.

"It is because of that understanding, however, they often do not have to. The oppressor looks into their eyes and sees the calm that grows out of the Warrior's depth of commitment. On some deep level, the oppressors' souls tremble, and they often back away and back down. Then, and only then, will the Warriors step their response down a notch. Or two. Or three."

He paused, looked around at everyone, took a deep breath, and continued.

"And they say a prayer of thanks for not having to kill. And when it is over they will laugh. Then will they go home, sit down, and cry.

"Whether they have fought and won, or whether the oppressor has backed down and left, the Warrior will laugh because they are still here. And they will cry because they are still here.

"Once again, they were left behind. Warriors know. Warriors, the ones who were called, who were created to do battle, are both condemned and blessed to a life of doing battle for the oppressed. For Warriors, the only real winner in battle is the Warrior who has 'crossed over the river and is resting in the shade of the tree.'

"It's sad to be left behind again, to know there are still more battles to fight. Look into the eyes of old Warriors and you will see it. In some ways the lucky ones are those who have gone on. They alone can rest now from a life of battles they never wanted in the first place."

There was a catch in Don's voice and then silence. I took my eyes off of the young woman's back and looked at him, and he was somewhere else. You could see it in his eyes. I glanced over at the woman kneeling beside him, and Jane was standing with him in that far away place as surely as they were sitting together this Sunday morning on the mats in the Dojo.

We sat, silent. Motionless. There was something holy in their sadness and the only proper response was to sit quietly, alone in the stillness with the others.

And I saw more clearly what they had been telling me. This place, this calling, these learnings are for the real world. I saw myself four months ago more clearly now, and some more of the pain slipped away.

He took a deep breath, let it out, relaxed a little, and then continued. "You have accepted the calling of Warrior that was laid out for you when God laid the cornerstones of the universe. It was no accident that you were born in the time that you were, in the place that you were, in the family that you were. You came here at this time, this place, for a purpose. You were not stamped out of a mold in some mass production line of souls.

"You were created as someone special. You were created for a special purpose. Before you were born, God knew your name, your *shem*—your power. God knew your name before your parents were born, or their parents, or their parents' parents. Your name was written in the Book of Warriors before time began. You have now arrived to take your place among us."

Jane continued, "When you were led here, you were both blessed and cursed. Blessed because you have found the path to yourself, your calling, and your power. And cursed, because you now join the ranks of those called to change the world. You were not called to be The Messiah of the World, but you are called to be a messiah to your part of it.

"Today you receive your Black Belt. It is not being given to you. It is being awarded to you because you earned it. You saw something in it before you even understood what that was, but you knew when you saw it, that it was yours for the claiming. So you chose a path that had already been trodden by generations of Warriors gone before.

"You began the quest, you faltered, you exalted, you were bored, you were discouraged, you cried, you laughed, and most of all, you hung in when you didn't think you could go any further. You did that during your test. You did that before your test.

"Believe me, these moments were only training grounds for the battles yet to come. They are not mere symbols, but are an intricate part of the process themselves. They are not milestones that you passed to get to this moment; they are the foundation of how you will be called on to do life. Maybe only once. Maybe again and again.

"But somewhere in this process, you reached a point where you couldn't go on, and then, inch by inch, second by second, you willed yourself past it and you went beyond.

"Learning that lesson was and is the goal of your training. It is the most important lesson you can take away from here. If there was any goal to be reached, any lesson to be learned, it is: 'you can go farther than you thought.' Remember that the next time you are down, hurting, bloodied, and without hope. You have been there before and your faith and your courage took you on. Faith appears while you are waiting for hope to come. Courage is the act of moving ahead based on that faith.

"Make no mistake. Courage is not a thing to be possessed. It is earned in moving beyond that which is hopeless, but must be done anyway. Courage is moving on when everyone else around you can no longer do anything but sit in the hopelessness of those who have given up."

Jane and Don stood up, turned, and picked up a Black Belt that had been sitting on a small stool. "This Black Belt we now present to you is not simply a reward nor is it to be seen as just a point of pride," she said. "It is also an acceptance and a reminder of your own death. By putting it on, you are accepting the responsibility for this process that you started before you understood who you really were. In accepting it, you are accepting that at any moment, you may be called upon to give up your life for that of someone else.

"This is your Black Belt. Now you are skilled enough to begin to learn what Warriors need to know. It is now time to remove the old belt and place the new one around you."

We all watched as Jenna stood, unwound the old brown belt off her waist, and then carefully accepted the folded belt from the hands of her two teachers. She wrapped it around her waist. At one point I swear I could feel fear starting to overwhelm her. Many others in the room shifted slightly, seeming to feel it also. Sitting still was hard to do; yet nobody moved.

And then the Black Belt was on and tied. The fear left as power flowed into her.

Don spoke again. "Wear this in practice, in ceremonies in the Dojo, and when testing students. But, do not go through the rest of life wearing it for others to see. The ones who need to come to you for protection will see it around you even as it hangs in your closet. The weak ones, the abusers, those who confuse control for power, will know it is around you from their fear of your power. Other than in practice you should leave it hanging out of sight. When you need to, take it out. Know that it is your salvation and your *shem*: your power and name. It is your life and your death.

"If evil comes fast, then act fast. But if evil is seen on the horizon, then put the belt around you or hold it in your hands while you contemplate doing battle. Make sure. Consult those you trust. Pray with it in your hands, and if you become sure that God has placed this battle in your path, then put it on, get between the oppressor and the victim, and don't run. Do only what you must, but do it without hesitation. And if by standing in that place, by standing on that line, it brings your death, die well.

"That day will be a good day to die. Make it a good death. Stand on the line and do not run. Take your place with the long line of other warriors who have gone before you:

"Be prepared to join them on the other side of the river.

"Be prepared to stay here for the next battle.

"Whichever happens, it is good and as it should be.

"Remember: Any time you as a Warrior are called to stand on the boundary line, you are doing what you were called to do before the universe was born.

"Go and live well, and because of you, may the world be a better place."

With that, the three of them stood and bowed to each other and then they both gave her a big hug.

She turned and bowed to the rest of us. We bowed back. There was an awkward moment of silence, and then applause and cheering broke out and a few moments later there was the sound of champagne corks popping.

I would have loved to slip out of the door so that I wouldn't have to face the others, but Jenna turned and looked straight at me. She ran across the room and jumped on me with both legs around my waist, her arms around my neck, and her mouth pressed against mine.

I stepped back to catch us, but the bench hit the back of my knee, my leg folded under me, and before I could adjust, we went down. I made an attempt to roll so it would at least look good. It didn't. We went down in a heap a heap of humanity – tangled arms and legs sticking out from some weird contortion of two bodies.

Laughing, she kissed me again and I fumbled around, embarrassed. Not only was there the class and Don and Jane to think about, but her parents were here also. Exuberance is part of what I love about her, but sometimes in the midst of the moment, I'm not always so sure.

We untangled as her family came up laughing, and waited for us as we got up. Her father stuck out his hand to me, "I'm Luis Moreno-Vargas and this is my wife, Carol. Carol's mother, Mrs. Hall. Our kids Hank, Rita, Liz, and Hank's friend Robbie", indicating each with a nod of his head. Before I could speak he turned to Jenna and with one eye-brow raised quizzically said to her, "I would hope that this is Les. If not, then I am going to be very confused."

She laughed and affirmed it. And then the class surged in and hugged and congratulated her.

Just as I stepped off to one side to give her time with the class, Don and Jane came up and introduced themselves to her parents and grand-mother. Her siblings were squeezed in with her in the mob over against one corner. Jane turned and spoke to me as though my being there was perfectly natural and it smoothed the way for me to be back without my feeling awkward.

The rest of the celebration is a blur now. I only remember from this far away in time: that I liked her family, was so proud of her and so in love with her that I hurt inside, and that somehow I had begun the next stage of healing just by coming back.

Most of the class had finally drifted away, and Jenna and I stood around trying to organize the car caravan to get her family back to her apartment. I thought that I was going to be able to get out without having to face either of the *sensei* by myself, but somehow, in the only split second that I was clear of others, Jane came up from behind and whispered in my ear.

"You belong here. This Wednesday night, 7:00 p.m. Come with Jenna. It's time for you to begin to find out who you really are. I can see it in your eyes. I can feel it. You're ready for the next stage, and eventu-ally, you will be able to lighten the burden you shouldered four months ago. No one can carry that alone and be whole. Come to us, Les. You belong here. Come back."

two

Laughter And Swords

In the fall of my twenty-second year, I whispered "Yes" to a question that I didn't even know had been asked. And in that moment, I stepped into a story that had been waiting for me to come along and live it. It wasn't just any story; it was my story. It had been spun for me by the Story Teller back in the time when Stories began and has been waiting for me across the ages. I suppose that it would be more accurate to say that I did not begin to live it. Rather, it began to live itself out in me early one Sunday morning, as I woke up ...

Although the sun hadn't fully peeked over the horizon, I could tell that it was going to be a spectacular day. The rain had ended in the night and the air was so clear I could almost make out individual leaves a whole mountain range away. It was the clarity that comes to the Blue Ridge only after a heavy rain takes the humidity out of the fall air. As I stumbled from bed, I felt an urge to find some hiking trails near my new home.

I had graduated from college, watched the last few embers of a love affair quietly die out in one final, sad conversation, gotten my first real job, and moved 500 miles away from anyone I knew. All in all, I guess it had been a pretty normal five months for a recently-used-to-be-college-student.

So, early this Sunday morning I started out. I decided to take along my neighbors' dog that I was watching for the weekend.

"Don't worry about a leash, if you don't want to," they said. "You can take him on a walk and he'll stay right with you."

They had been right to a point. He stayed with me while we were in the car and while we were walking up the fire-road with him at the end of the leash. He hadn't even pulled on it once. So I let him off of it part of the way up. He sat there very nicely. Then, while I was relieving myself, he simply took off, straight up the mountain. I couldn't believe it. That dumb mutt just ran off up the hill and left me holding a leash with no dog attached!

After the initial shock and frustration, I realized that I didn't really need to be all that upset. I had wanted to take a long walk today anyway, so this would be it. If I didn't find him, then my neighbors would have to. After all, it was their idea to let him off the leash. So I looked around, got my bearings, and started bushwhacking up the hillside after him.

After about fifteen minutes of trudging through the brush, I got my second wind. Shortly after that, I noticed "Posted" signs on some trees up ahead. I remember grumbling to myself, "Great! I'm going to get shot for getting too near to someone's still or marijuana patch, all because my neighbor's dog ran off."

I ignored the signs and went on past the line, marked by an old barbed wire fence with most of its sections lying rusted on the ground. I got about three steps past the fence when an uneasiness came over me.

Something didn't feel right, so I went back down to the fence to look around. I couldn't find anything unusual; shrugging my shoulders, I turned to start back up the hill. Then one of the posted signs caught my attention and I read it. What kind of a posted sign was that, anyway? I figured that the signs must have been what gave me such a weird feeling.

PRIVATE PROPERTY
PLEASE RESPECT THE BOUNDARIES

IF YOU NEED TO ENTER,
DO SO WITH
GENTLENESS FOR THE LAND,
RESPECT FOR THE PRIVACY OF ANYONE
YOU HAPPEN TO MEET.
AND PLEASE FEEL FREE,
TO BE THE BEST OF YOURSELF.
W-P²

Sundays in the Dojo | 15

With the sun rising well over the top of the mountain, the sky was getting lighter. As I turned back toward the peak, I heard the laughter. I stepped back over a downed section of fence and plodded uphill toward the distant sound. I didn't know exactly where the dog had gone, but he had headed in this general direction and maybe he would be as drawn toward the laughter, as I was. I ran across a small trail that zigzagged its way up the mountain and took it, to avoid the underbrush.

Twenty minutes later the trail ended in a clearing. As I turned the last bend I saw a ten- or twelve-sided building, maybe twenty-five or thirty feet across. It was one story, with walls that were ten to twelve feet high. The roof was probably twenty-five feet high or more in the center, where all the sections came together. There were large skylights in each section. The walls were a varnished natural wood and there were large windows in each section of wall, with the exception of the section with the extension and double glass doors.

The trail entered the meadow a little off to one side and slightly behind the doors, which were standing open. A man and a woman, both dressed all in black, were standing in front of them, with their backs to me. They were wearing some kind of martial arts outfit with long, flowing skirts. Standing completely still and hands folded in a prayer position, they were breathing slowly and in synch.

All of a sudden I felt dizzy and realized I was losing my balance. Actually, it felt as though reality was swirling and I was standing still. Instinctively, I stuck out my hand to grab onto a tree. The rough feel of the bark and the support of a tree trunk stabilized me somewhat. At least I didn't feel like I was going to fall over in the next few seconds.

But just as I began to feel in control, I was drawn right back into a vortex of a reality that just wouldn't sit still. In my dizziness I had missed something. Their hands had moved so naturally and so smoothly, that it wasn't until I saw the swords flashing out of their scabbards that I realized that they were moving. I hadn't even noticed they were wearing swords. At that same instant I heard the chant – or prayer – or something:

"I am an old Warrior …"

And the swords were held out in front of them in some kind of two handed, on-guard posture. Then movement and sound came together again and ended with the swords held in one hand and extended straight up.

"Come from across the centuries ..."

And they moved again, pointing their swords to the ground as they turned and faced each other smiling, and with great tenderness said:

"To stand beside you in this life, this time ..."

Turning back-to-back and extending their arms open wide:

"To proclaim good news to the discouraged ..."

Their swords glinted in the light as they swung them around behind their backs to stop them parallel to the ground and their left hands were out in front of them as if giving a blessing:

"To heal the wounded and broken ..."

With a sudden step forward their swords came from behind their backs and slashed down diagonally in front of them. There was a certainty in the move and a sureness in their voices that gave me a start:

"To protect the innocent and bring freedom to the captives ..."

The swords flashed again, swinging across their bodies, ending with the tips in their left hand. Then the sheath slid up over the sword and both were slowly slid back into their belts. Their hands came free, their arms extended and their palms and faces turned upward and the final words were spoken with a quiet joy:

"And life to all who seek it."

And so they stood, as still as the time they were in. Then it was over. They slowly lowered their arms and turned to walk into the building. Just before they entered, they glanced at each other and then turned and looked straight at me.

"Hello," the woman said. They looked at me—or rather through me—for what seemed like a really long time. And smiled. Really smiled.

"You must be the one we were waiting for," the man said. There was another long pause while they waited for me to gain some grasp on reality.

Finally, I started to feel a little normal and then it hit me. They were old. They had moved so smoothly that I had just assumed that they were young – but they were an old couple. He had a white beard and her hair was mostly silver, but I hadn't noticed any of this during the whole ritual. I stared at them with total surprise. I tried to cover my rudeness and blurted out, "I'm sorry. It's just that, well, it's just that you're old. I mean, I didn't realize that until just now ..."

Oh God! What had I said? I wanted to turn and run, but my legs couldn't obey. So I stood there, as rooted into the ground as the tree I was leaning on.

Their laughter was instantaneous and loud, but with no hint of derision. It was just pure enjoyment of the moment. She spoke in a soft Southern lilt, "Well, as old as two people in their fifties can be, but not as old as we hope to be someday. Come on in and rest." There was a pause. "You need a break."

I found myself sitting on a bench inside the building without knowing how I got there. I was petting my neighbor's dog and the man was pouring me a glass of water from a ceramic jug. I came to my senses thinking, "They have got to be W-P2, whatever that is."

They left me to sit and collect what was left of my wits while they began their workout. There was a series of stretches and moves, most of which looked like some variation on karate moves I'd seen in the movies. They moved on to rolls and falls and soon were flying through the air and landing with loud thumps that I could feel through the floor. About fifteen minutes in, they removed the flowing skirts that I later learned were called *hakamas*. They started doing a series of moves that looked like defenses; blocks followed by kicks or hand strikes.

During the time they were working out I had time to study them. I would often catch myself staring at one or the other, but if they noticed they didn't let on. It certainly didn't change their mood. There was a different feel than in the few Dojos I had been in before. They were more relaxed, laughed a lot, and bantered back and forth. But there was a strange combination of relaxation and concentration each time they did any move. They had to have been doing them a long time.

She was a medium height and build. Her hair had been dark brown or black but was mostly silver now. It was probably shoulder-length hair, but was tied back and folded up into a bun. She had a smooth complexion and didn't seem to be wearing any makeup. For an older lady, she was quite attractive.

He was large. He was also very fast, which was an unexpected combination. His hair was mostly brown with some tips of silver at the temples. His beard was full, but neatly trimmed and completely white. It was a stark contrast with the black uniform he was wearing.

Their uniforms were all black, including the flowing skirts that they had been wearing. The belts around their waists were red with a black stripe running the full length of the belt. They were wearing some kind of sneaker that had a very thin sole. It didn't seem to slow them down from the spins and turns they did with so little effort.

The rhythm changed when their warmup ended. "Three or four from the front." was her reply to his unasked question of what she wanted. He calmly stood there awhile. Then with no warning, he grabbed her collar and tried to hit her in the face with his other fist. My breath was caught by the lack of warning, the speed and the seriousness of the attack. I think I let out a loud gasp.

I wasn't even sure of what I saw, but it looked like she actually ran into him with her arm in the air. She knocked him sideways, wrapped her arm around his neck and then her leg shot up in between his and he went flying. He landed with another of those awful sounding thumps. After just a split second of not moving, he got up and faced her.

She was turned partly toward me and I could see her face. There was not even a hint of the kindness I had seen up to that point. No laughter. No smile. Nothing but some really calm, really deep level of commitment to what was happening.

There was some serious shit going on here and I felt the fear rising. It had started in my stomach and then spread quickly all over me. Looking back, I know now that I hadn't been afraid of *them*; I had just been afraid. It was really scary to even be in the area with something like this going on.

Then he was on her again, this time with both hands grabbing her throat, hitting her so hard it knocked her backward. I reacted with a wave of nausea as she seemed to melt or something. One moment she was apparently falling over backwards and the next moment she was standing a little to one side with her back to him. Before my brain could realize what my body was reacting to, it was over. She appeared to crumple, but then he was upside down and landing hard on the mat. She was standing up straight now. I could see the red marks on her throat. The attack had been for real. So had the response.

But he got up again. He was a big man; probably six feet and 225 pounds. He just ran right into her side with his chest, grabbing one breast and wrapping his other arm around her back. This time she crumpled for real and went down. I was reeling. But just as her knee hit the mat she gave a quick turn and he landed on the mat – hard. She was kneeling over him and gave a loud shout and drove her knuckles, upside down, full speed toward his throat. She stopped an inch away. This time he didn't get up. His face was tense and his eyes were squinted shut from pain. He rolled slowly from one side to the other and then back again. He gently began to move his shoulders.

"Are you okay?" She was obviously worried.

"Yeah. I'm getting too old for this crap. God! That one hurt. It was just so low that I couldn't get all the way over before I hit, so I took it a little on one shoulder and couldn't slap hard enough. I'll be okay in a minute."

"I'm really sorry. The way you hit me I was going down hard into the 'broken collar bone' position, so all I could do was turn as I went. I wasn't really keen on landing like that."

"No problem. I certainly hadn't planned for it to go that way. Man! I do not like those low-level falls anymore." He was moving his shoulders around carefully. "Actually, I don't think that I ever did like them. I just used to get up from them quicker." He looked over at her slowly, "You had to do it though, or you really would have gotten badly hurt."

He rolled over and worked up to his hands and knees. He then sat back onto his knees and slowly stretched his shoulders a few more times. Then he got up and did several other slow stretches. He didn't seem injured, but he was hurting.

"Five-minute break," he announced. He looked at me and smiled, "For an old man to put the pieces back together." She laughed at his comment and turned and smiled at me. Her smile made me feel totally relaxed in their presence again, but her sideways glance at him told me she was double-checking just to make sure he really was all right.

He was moving around a bit more smoothly. "It's that rib again," he said. "Can you put it back in for me?" He lay face down on the floor with his arms folded under his chest. She straddled him, bent over, and held her right wrist with her left hand. She put a fist on his back just off center and then began to push hard. After a few moments she released quickly. She repeated the process. He moved around a bit and said, "That got it." He rolled back into the same position. She then pushed down on his back with her fists on either side of his spinal column and I could hear the popping sound from where I was. He groaned and I saw the tension release from his body. He got up much more quickly and said, "Thanks. I actually think I might make it. We'll have to go a little easier for the moment."

She nodded and said, "Okay. It's my turn." In response to his request, she went over to a cabinet on one of the walls and came back with a rubber gun and knife and a lightweight plastic club. She put the gun in her belt, laid the club on at the side of the mat, and then suddenly crouched, holding the knife at her side. That mood was back in both of them. I knew that it didn't make any sense, but I felt the same fear rising in me again.

She slashed at him several times. Each time he barely got out of the way, but it seemed more like not wasting energy rather than almost getting cut. Suddenly, as she slashed high, he seized her arm, somehow wound up behind her, and then grabbed the back of her neck and drove her to her knees. Her hand was still holding the knife, which was shoved into her stomach. I felt sick again.

She got back up and slashed again. This time he danced out of the way as he grabbed her hand. Again, a quick movement, but this time the rubber knife blade sliced across her throat. She stepped back and dropped the knife acknowledging his win, but suddenly the gun was coming out of her belt. Just as it came level, he had grabbed hold of her hand and there was this blur of motion. He seemed to simultaneously kick her groin and twist her arm. She went down and he stepped back and with the gun in his hand, aiming it right at her.

She rolled to the edge of the mat and grabbed the club. He threw the gun to the side as she swung the club backhand at his head. Another blur and he wound up behind her with the club in his hand swinging it toward the back of her head. He stopped an inch away.

He moved away. With a shrug of his shoulders he said, "I think that's it for today. That rib is out again." He lay back down and she put it back in for him.

They moved to the center of the mat and knelt down. They spent several minutes in total quiet, meditating, and then got up and came over and sat down next to me.

We introduced ourselves and then talked for a few minutes. In response to my questions about W-P2 I was told that it stood for

Warrior-Priest, which was the rank that both of them were. I was invited to stay for class, which was to start in about thirty minutes. I was given the choice of sitting and watching or participating in it, whichever appealed to me. As we waited, I found myself telling them about my recent past and a fair amount of my not-so-recent past.

And with that, my Sundays in the Dojo began.

three

Orange Belt

One Person, Unarmed, Stationary

FINDING A HOME

As I look back from so many years on down the road, Ted, I am often surprised that the first few weeks at the Dojo sometimes seem so clearly imprinted in my memory. I guess that on some level I knew that I was stepping into a new chapter of life and that nothing would ever be the same again.

After meeting Don and Jane, I sat around waiting. People straggled in during the next half-hour. Some were already in their workout clothes. Others changed when they got there—in the main room, oblivious to everyone else. I later found the bathroom, a small add-on room off the Dojo

There were about twenty-five to thirty people in the class, and they were quite a mix. Some were younger, some middle aged, and there was even one lady who had to be in her late sixties or early seventies. Most were in very good physical condition, but a few ranged from slightly out of shape to having enough shape for two people. What was most fascinating was the social mix. It ranged from business people to construction types, with a few others that seemed like old hippies. There was a wide range of outfits, from shorts to sweats or leotards. Many took out gis or pieces of uniforms and laid them to one side. Among those with uniforms, there was a rainbow of colored belts.

There was lots of noise and laughter as people did their own warming up. Then a barely audible, low, bell-like sound came from the front of the Dojo. People moved into rows and knelt with their hands on their knees. One woman sat down stiffly into sort of a sidesaddle position and leaned against the wall.

I joined them, and everyone's breathing soon synchronized. I felt reality starting to swirl again, but this time I wasn't concerned. I felt safer with them now. Besides, I was kneeling on the mat. How far could I fall?

Another ring of the bell and everyone stood, almost in unison. One person helped the woman in the sidesaddle position to stand up. They let the woman hold on until she signaled that she was steady and could be left to stand on her own. Don and Jane waited as though there was no delay, and then the exercises started. I tried to learn them as I went. One of the students, wearing a Blue Belt, had moved back next to me and helped me approximate the moves the others were doing.

The stretches went fine. Abdominals were tough, and I made it only part way through. I knew I wasn't the only one not completing them, judging by the grunts and moans from some others. Push-ups were just plain weird. Everyone got down into the normal position but then stuck their butts up in the air. Don spoke directly to me: "Les. Do you have any rotator cuff or a.c. joint injuries? No? Okay. Go ahead … and watch your nose."

I got into the "V" position and then followed the class going straight down, then straightening my body out only a few inches from the floor, then arching my back and putting my head up, then straightening back out, and then back up—well, at least until my arms gave out suddenly and I found out why he told me to watch my nose.

Soon we were into rolls, and the student who had helped me through my exercises took me off to one corner of the mat and helped me roll gently while sitting down. The others were soon leaping, jumping, and smashing into the mat. Some got up with pained expressions, some with smiles, some with no response—as if this were the most natural thing in the world—and some with a sense of deep joy.

Occasionally, there was a particular sound to a landing and everyone would groan, and then there would be laughter. It was strange, though; no one was made fun of. It was just the laughter that comes from having been there before, of having lived through the jolt and the pain, and knowing that you would be there again in the future. It was a laughter that took off the edge.

Then the bell sounded. Everyone moved to one end of the Dojo and the mats were folded and moved out of the way. People began to move up and down the floor in unison. At first there were just leg movements. A little while later, blocks and blows were added. Don and Jane went to the cabinet and handed six-foot staffs (which, I soon learned, were called *bo*) to a few people. They held these behind their backs at hip level and did the stances up and back. It made the mistakes in their movements really obvious. No one offered me one. I suppose that my mistakes were obvious enough.

The mats were put back down. Don called out a Japanese-sounding name and two students came to the mats. They bowed and then grabbed hold of each other's gi tops. Others, who weren't wearing any, went and got theirs and put their belts on. One student called out the same name and the other repeated it. Then the first student threw the second one. They did this again, but to the other side. They bowed and one left the mat; the one who was thrown turned and took her place. This continued through the line. A few of the beginners didn't throw anyone themselves, but were thrown by an upper belt student who handled them gently and carefully. In one case they practically placed the beginner on the mat and then corrected his landing position. They ran through several more sets of throws while I sat and watched.

Then the bell sounded again and students went through the line the same way, only this time doing defenses. Jane would call out the name of an attack and everyone would do this several times. Jane or Don stood by, passing out compliments and adjusting moves as needed. The beginners all looked pretty similar in their moves, but the advanced students used really different techniques from each other. Some used mostly strikes and kicks, while others used mostly holds or throws. I was shown something different than what the others were practicing. The same advanced student, Jenna (yes, Ted, this was your grandmother), showed me a wrist release that was simple and amazingly effective. She then showed me several more moves.

The bell sounded again and people ringed the mat. One person was invited into the center of what they called a defense circle. Don stood behind the victim and pointed at different people and made a gesture as to what kind of attack they should do. With beginners the attacks went slowly and their responses were slow. With the advanced students only other advanced students surrounded them. Good thing; these attacks were much faster and more in earnest. The responses were just as serious. People threw blows that stopped an inch or two away and a lot of people went flying through the air or dropped really fast and hard on the mat at the end of someone's defense. Although I was glad that I wasn't one of the advanced students, I knew that I really wanted to be among them. After everyone had been in the circle for one or two minutes, the bell rang again.

There were a few slow stretches, some more meditation, and then everyone rose and recited the words from a poster on the wall, titled "Code of Ethics":

DO NOT CONFRONT WHERE RESOLUTION IS POSSIBLE.

DO NOT ATTACK WHERE
CONFRONTATION WILL WORK.

DO NOT BLOCK WHERE DEFLECTION WILL WORK.

DO NOT CAUSE PAIN WHERE CONFUSION
OR RESTRAINT WILL WORK.

CAUSE PAIN OVER INJURY,
AND MAIMING OVER KILLING.

DO ONLY WHAT HURT YOU MUST –
ANYTHING ELSE IS VIOLENT AND YOU WILL
HAVE BECOME AS THE ATTACKER.

DO NOT DO LESS THAN YOU MUST—YOU WILL
HAVE LEFT A VICTIM DEFENSELESS AND A VIOLENT
PERSON UNAWARE OF THE NEED FOR CHANGE.

They all bowed and then it was over. People left the same way they came in. Some left in a hurry, some lingered and talked with each other, and some asked Don or Jane a question. Jane asked me to stay around if I had time. I had plenty of that, so I was still there a half-hour later when the next-to-last person left. Jane came over and introduced me to Leroy, a young man about my age. She told me that they were glad I had come and that Leroy had agreed to bring me back next week. She looked at me, smiled, and said, "You belong here." Leroy offered to drive me and the dog back to my car, and I took him up on it.

I felt elated. For some reason, Jane's statement that I belonged there gave me a real high. I didn't think to ask her why she had said that. I would have felt lucky just to be allowed to come back. But to be told that I belonged ...

Two days after that first Sunday, Leroy called me and gave me directions to an elementary school and said he would meet me there thirty minutes before class was to start. So the next Sunday, I drove out to the base of the mountain, found the school, and pulled into the parking lot.

There were several empty cars there already, and people were busily getting into two other cars. While three people were crowding into the back seat of his old Honda Civic, Leroy explained that there was limited space for parking at the Dojo.

After several miles of climbing up a well maintained, but winding state road, we turned off onto a private drive and crossed an iron bridge over a creek. After a few twists and turns we went past a walled courtyard with an ungated driveway that led into the back of a house. The view from the front of the house would overlook both the valley and the mountains beyond and must have been spectacular.

A short way past the courtyard, the cars began to park along the road. A few car-lengths down, the road ended at a small meadow with a short path leading from it to the front of the Dojo. It came into the clearing almost directly opposite from where I had come in the previous week.

We went into the Dojo with everyone bowing as they entered the door. Don and Jane, the *sensei* (teachers), were there, and people were warming up on their own. Don and Jane smiled and welcomed everyone as they came in. I felt the same warmth and invitation I had last Sunday. The class started the same way it had the last week. To my surprise and pleasure, Jenna, the same student, was assigned to work with me. She was stunning, and I certainly had no objections to being with her for most of the class.

Jenna reviewed with me the rolls that I had learned the previous week and added one more. While I found them quite simple to do, I did not yet roll with the ease of most of the others. After the warmups were over, Jenna worked me on several new defenses, including escape from a bear hug, both front and back.

In the process of learning bear-hug defenses, I picked up several new blows and ways of using my hands and feet as striking weapons. I also picked up on the idea that I really liked being hugged by, or hugging Jenna, even if she could have killed me or was striking at my groin and stopping just inches away.

Then she showed me the gate-swing move in more detail. Jenna explained that just like a heavy gate could swing easily on a hinge, we can also pivot easily if we are centered, and swing on the ball of one foot. The idea was for me not to stay rigid, but relaxed, and to find the center of my body no matter what position I was in. Then, staying balanced, I just swung around on one foot to the front or the back. It looked so easy when she did it, but it felt awkward to me, so I just tried harder.

"Les, you have to relax into this," she said. "Hard work won't get you there. *Fun* work will. The harder you try to look good or feel coordinated, the worse you will do. The less you care about how you look, or even if it works at all, the more likely it will be to just happen."

It sounded logical, but I was the least trained individual in the class, being taught by one of the best students in the class, who happened to be a young woman about my age, and who also was really something to look at. Testosterone just doesn't let you relax in that kind of a situation. So I tried to pretend that it didn't matter. That didn't work either, but it was the best option I had in my repertoire at that age.

What really sold me on the system, though, was how you used the gate swing when attacked. If someone pushed on your left shoulder from the front, you relaxed just enough, shifted your weight slightly to your right side, pivoted on the ball of your right foot, and then let their force move you out of the way.

Suddenly you weren't in front of them, but were standing to the side. If they pushed from behind, you swung forward. Jenna then showed me how you could pivot more than once and wind up behind them or anywhere else you wanted to be.

My mind flashed back to the previous week, when Don had attacked his wife so hard and she seemed to melt in front of him. It started to make sense. It wasn't magic or Oriental mysticism … It was simply physics and anatomy.

"So how do you make someone fall?"

Jenna laughed. "Just get out of their way, help them keep going the way they are already going, and then get back in the way of something of theirs, such as a leg, just when they were going to move it to catch their balance."

"And, of course, there are ways to do this really well."

She laughed again, "Absolutely. Have you ever seen Jane throw someone from a front choke attack?" I thought back to last week and that awful thud of Don's body hitting the mats. "Yes? Well, that works better for women than men. When choked from the front, men usually do a similar gate swing move, but then respond with an elbow blow.

"Because our centers of gravity are different, women can throw easier from that position than we can hit. That's why people often think that women can't fight as well as men can—because usually we are taught to fight like a man and not to fight like a woman. Jane and Don say that they tripped over that issue a lot when they were first teaching, years ago. They finally figured out what the problem was and then began to work on each technique to make shifts. Now women are taught to do some techniques differently, taught some techniques that men aren't and vice versa, and taught some of them in a different order than men are.

"But we all use the same basic principle: 'Win by yielding.'

"Another concept that we use is: 'Use your strengths against their weaknesses. Never fight strength on strength if you don't have to.'" She smiled impishly and glanced up at me. "Unless of course, you're a male trying to prove something to yourself. Even then it's not a good idea, but in the teenage years it may be unavoidable. So much for the theory. Let's get back to work."

After the class was finished practicing a few more techniques, they turned to the front at the sound of the bell and broke into groups by skill levels. Each group had a teacher, and one or two new techniques were demonstrated and practiced. This day there was no defense circle.

I figured out after several classes that this was a pattern: Defense circle and talks on different topics on even-numbered Sundays, and new techniques on the odd-numbered Sundays.

Then we lined up, recited the Code of Ethics, bowed, and got back into the cars over a period of twenty minutes. I said goodbye to Leroy at the parking lot, made arrangements to meet him there the next week, and headed home, feeling exhilarated and thrilled.

I wasn't sure if the excitement was the jujitsu or Jenna—especially the body contact with Jenna. There was something really different about being in contact with a woman who was comfortable in her body. It was also different to be physically in contact with a woman in a non-dating and non-sexual setting.

It sounds confusing, but it was both very sensual and very sexual, in a sort of a non-sexy kind of a way. I mean, how sexy could it be to be touching a woman who was getting ready to smash your body onto a mat at a high rate of speed? Or maybe it was because the contact was all about fighting, and she was so relaxed with even the full-body contact of a bear hug ...

I realized with a start that while I had been thinking of certain techniques other than jujitsu, and about other types of body contact; I had completely missed the exit toward my home.

It was worth it. Although the specifics of my musings that day have left me over the years, the feeling I had then is still in me, in every part of me, as I write these words today.

four

Orange Belt Sessions

Middle Weeks

Somewhere in the first three or four weeks, I had learned the first of a number of stances. Well, actually they called them stages or pauses, but the karate style I had studied for a while called them stances. Jenna taught me how to stand in them, what their strong and weak lines were, how to move in them, and what their uses were.

I asked Don at one point why I rarely saw him use any of these. His response was typical of how both he and Jane taught. He gave me just enough of an answer for my level and then invited me to flesh it out. He told me that he used them all the time. They were just stages that he moved through while defending. In some other cases, they were pauses where he stopped momentarily.

He said that he never stayed long in them as a general rule, and then explained a concept that I heard over and over in my training: "It's all about function. Use them when you need to and don't when you don't. If they work in a given situation, use them. Shoot, if it would work best to be in one for five minutes straight, then stay in it for five minutes straight. Just stay alive."

This made a great deal of sense to me. It explained their view of form. The second or third week I asked Jenna if my form was correct on one of the blows and her response was, "Yes. It seems to work well for you."

"Yes, but is it correct?"

Her brow furrowed a bit as she thought it over, and then nodded toward the side of the mat near Jane, went over and sat down. She motioned me to do the same.

"Form always follows function, Les. We could work on getting your form just right by some set standard, but it would take years for you to make it functional on a basic level. And it wouldn't be *your* best form, just your best attempt at some abstract concept of the best form. And that's okay in ballet or in a martial art that emphasizes *kata* (form). It's not okay in our system, where it is strictly self-protection and the goal is to stay alive. On any given day your form may be slightly different. As you get more advanced, your form will become more set. This may seem paradoxical, however.

"To a beginner it will look more and more like an upper belt's form, but from the view of an advanced student of the art, we will see that you are getting more and more individualized. Whatever form allows you to hit the fastest and hardest and most accurately is the correct form. As you become more comfortable with the move you will start to notice problems with it, and then you will be ready to advance to a better way of doing it."

"But if you have practiced it the wrong way, then wouldn't it be harder to change?" I asked. This seemed backwards to everything that I had been taught in gym class, my former karate class, and even in my engineering classes: "Focus on doing it right the first time or pay the price later."

"Not really, Les." Jane joined in. She sat down on the mat next to us. "The method or style of a given technique that we teach everyone is the easiest way to do a technique for a beginning student. It's sort of a statistical crapshoot. It works for most people, but if that way doesn't work for a specific person, then we immediately switch to something else. But most importantly, we want the technique to feel right to you. So you learn a blow and you do it well. After a while, you find that it doesn't quite feel right, so we modify it. Now it feels better all at once, and your body has been looking for this feeling. It will quickly pick it up and won't go back to what is uncomfortable.

"The body, quite rightly, does what feels good, not what feels bad or uncomfortable. Often in our society we have learned to force our body into patterns that don't work or match who we really are. That's when real trouble starts. Trust me: You will learn much faster and easier this way, and you will be an effective fighter more quickly. Our goal is to make you a better fighter each time you come here. Each time you should leave having learned something that makes you better at defend— JOHN! FREEZE!"

Her head had suddenly snapped around and she focused on a pair of people wrestling on the mat as she snapped out that very sharp command. She was up and moving toward them as she spoke. Don's head had spun toward the pair at the sound of Jane's voice, but he relaxed and turned back to those he was working with.

"What was that about?"

Jenna shook her head and laughed. "Those three guys, the one standing and the two wrestling, are something. They are always trying something they have seen somewhere, but haven't been taught." Her smile turned more serious. "This time they were way over their heads. They could have done some real damage to each other. Jane stopped it before they got close to doing real harm."

"I didn't realize that she was watching them. I thought she was focused on us."

She shook her head and gave a quick laugh. "You'll get used to it. She was completely focused on us, but then something serious happened elsewhere and she saw it. She reacted to keep it from happening. She and Don are both this way. They will be focused completely on someone and yet, at the same time, they will also be completely aware of everything around them. I'm nowhere close to them, but I've noticed that the longer I've trained here, the more I get like that. I'll see things that I don't notice, at least on the surface, until something seems wrong, and then suddenly I realize that I have been aware of it for some time. The strange thing is that the more aware of my surroundings I become, the less nervous I am. You would think that you would become more anxious the more you realize what can happen, but, in truth, you get more relaxed."

"So the gate swing, the blows, the defenses are all just starting points?" The engineer in me was feeling really ungrounded. "What is your norm? How do I know where I'm headed?"

"You want to work toward doing things better, more effectively, having more fun with them ..." There was a pause and then she suddenly got excited. "It's like falling from a throw. At first it's scary. Then you do one that's right and it feels wonderful. Then somewhere along the line you'll lose focus, get sloppy, and boy, will you pay for it! You won't get harmed, but it will hurt.

"But somewhere along the line …" her face began to light up, and she looked away as if trying to find the words. "… somewhere it just becomes fun. And you start feeling the whole process of the fall. It isn't just one move and you're down. You can feel all of it and the rush of being upside down in the air and moving so fast is just great. I mean, the landing is like it isn't even there. You hit and you're back up, wanting to do it again. It's the ultimate roller coaster ride."

Her voice got louder and more intense; she picked up speed. "I remember shortly after it happened to me the first time, Les. Just for fun, Don showed us a totally useless form of the circle throw, but one where you could throw someone upside down a really long way. We got to running at each other and then being thrown, just to see how far we could go in the air. Jane showed up with some masking tape and a tape measure. We just threw and flew, and threw and flew, over and over. That's all we did for the whole class."

She reached over and grabbed my forearm in excitement. "Les, I went over eighteen feet in the air, upside down! And then when I landed I did a shoulder roll, and then another because of the momentum, and then collided into Jane who grabbed me and rolled me sideways. It was kind of a jolt and we ended up in a heap, but she was laughing. I asked if she was okay and she just nodded her head toward one side. I looked up. If she hadn't stopped me I would have rolled right into one of the windows. She and I just lay there and laughed and laughed until the tears came. God, I felt alive!

"Les. They aren't teaching you martial arts here. These aren't jujitsu principles you're learning."

I felt a start and a queasy feeling in my stomach. What were they teaching us? There was a serious tone to her voice, but she continued before I could even formulate my thoughts.

"They are teaching us how to live life. These aren't just jujitsu principles, they are life principles. They are how you to do life: 'Get out of the way of an attack', 'See trouble before it starts.' You can do this in everyday life. I am only beginning to learn how to do this in the rest of my world, but this is really good stuff."

It was at that moment, watching her excitement, that I knew that this was more than just liking to work out with this woman; this was the beginning of my love for her. What scared me was that I didn't know whether it was anything to her other than just another student to teach. I didn't know if her excitement was more about the Dojo than me. I felt a sense of worry, wondering if I would lose her before I had even begun to connect with her.

"You okay?" she said. "You look worried. I didn't mean to ... I just got carried away."

"It's okay. I'm fine. I just went inside myself for a moment. I ..."

The bowl sounded for us to get together for the end of class. As I stood up and moved into line, I noticed both Don and Jane looking our way, but they were turning and moving toward the front of the class, so I missed their response.

I went back home quietly this time, and that Sunday afternoon was a long one. I kept trying to find a way to hope that it wouldn't hurt if it didn't work out with Jenna and me.

Jenna and me? There was no "Jenna and me"—just me, hoping for something more. I didn't even know what she did or where she lived or if she dated or was engaged or married. I made up my mind to find out, and with a whole herd of butterflies in my stomach, I picked up the phone and called Leroy.

LAST WEEKS

Almost three months had gone by, and several other students and I were reviewing for the upcoming Orange Belt test. I was amazed at how much I had picked up in that short time. We had learned the skeleton that the rest of the system was going to hang on. We learned all of the defenses for attacks from one unarmed person. They were all done standing still, which seemed a little strange. But it made sense once Jane had told us, "It's rare that you'll be attacked by someone standing still. After all, if they did, then you could just walk away. It's just that it's easier to learn this way at first, when you aren't trying to time the opponent's moves with yours. This is going to be the main work for Green Belt; you'll work on these same moves, but with both of you moving."

The other thing that I realized was how much applied theory I had learned. I had also begun to understand what Jenna was talking about.

There were a couple of times at work that I noticed something was not quite right, and I was able to avoid trouble or at least being in an uncomfortable situation. One time I saw our project manager from a distance and realized that he must have had a rough day and was in a bad mood.

Twenty minutes later I saw him getting ready to leave my boss's office, halfway down the hall I was in. He was a good guy and I wouldn't have gotten into any trouble from him, but I figured, why be associated with a bad day? So I casually shifted my path to a more circuitous route in order to keep from running into him. Why put myself into a potential line of fire if I didn't have to?

I doubt that I saved myself from anything at all, but it was nice to be that aware and be more in control. Then, two days later when I saw him again and he was back to his normal, upbeat self, I continued a path that went by him, said hello, and went on my way. Definitely a less stressful way to do life.

The "vocabulary method" of defense was also beginning to make sense. I had now learned a base amount of "verbs" and "nouns" and could begin to put the sentences together. Instead of just doing a wrist release, I now could do a blow, then the release, and then follow up in one of a variety of ways. I felt good about what I had learned and how fast it was going.

I also felt awkward at how klutzy and slow I felt doing these defenses when compared to the advanced students. My one positive thought that kept me going was, that on some level, I must have been doing okay, because I had caught up with several people who had started several months earlier than I had.

Leroy and I had taken to riding together, and because we lived so close, we would take turns picking each other up for class. He was fascinating, and we began to hang out some between classes. Like most of the people at the Dojo he was an unusual mix. He was a senior in college and double majoring in dance and marketing.

These majors might make sense from a theoretical, business point of view, but there aren't that many people out there that can pull off such a strange combination. He was studying for his Green Belt test and was beautiful to watch. His moves were so smooth and fluid, and he was such a quick study; that dancing background really helped. It turned out that Jenna was also a dance major who had just graduated last year.

She and Leroy had met at the college and she was the one who had brought him to the Dojo. He and Jenna were planning to go into business together and open a dance school, once he graduated.

Right now, she was working as an office secretary during the day and as a dance instructor for the rec department at night and on weekends. They estimated that they would have to wait for eighteen months to two years after Leroy graduated to get enough money together in order to open their own school. They were saving everything they could to get to this goal. Leroy's partner of two years was already out of school, working as an accountant, and hoping to pass his CPA exam soon. He might also put up some of the money when the time came.

But the best news I had gotten from Leroy was that Jenna wasn't seeing anyone. Unfortunately, after the first few weeks, she didn't actually teach me, as she was working out on her own stuff. Within those several weeks I had gotten enough background that I could join several others who were studying Orange Belt, and we were taught as a group.

Still, I got to see her and we talked some. I really wanted to meet outside of class but was having doubts as to how to proceed. The chance I was waiting for didn't open up until after the Orange Belt test, which I passed with flying colors, but still felt inferior somehow.

It was hard trying to wait to ask her out, but I was too afraid of messing things up to push ahead. So, I just kept coming and watching. Her skill level fascinated me. Just like Leroy, she was a really fast study and was so smooth in her moves. I would watch as much as I could, while either Don or Jane would work one-on-one with her.

The defense part of the Blue Belt test was to defend against an armed attack by one person. The gun defense seemed easy and the club didn't seem that hard, although you had to be really fast for either of them to work. You have a very narrow margin of error with a weapon. Those defenses were practiced over and over. It was amazing to watch.

Sometimes she would "get killed" in the first few seconds. Other times she held out against a knife or club for a minute or so. Sometimes she nailed them in just a few seconds. As much as I enjoyed watching her whenever I could sneak the time from my practice, I found that same fear rising in me that had happened my first time at the Dojo. It often held on for several days and really depressed me.

I mentioned it to Leroy one night.

"Does it have to do with it being Jenna who's being attacked, Les?"

"Not really. At least I don't think so. It happened that first time I was here and watched Don and Jane work out. It's happened with others, too. There's something deep inside that really bothers me. I feel emotionally gutted."

He thought awhile and then said, "I'm no counselor, but is it touching some old memory?"

At least some of that answer was easy. "No. My home was pretty good, growing up. Mom was a little too much of a Martha Stewart to be completely comfortable with the mess kids leave around, but nothing too out of line. No violence, not even verbal. Dad was fine. I mean, I knew better than to push the boundary too far, but I never felt any fear of being hurt. I felt afraid once or twice when I talked back to Mom. But it was the normal fear any thirteen- or fourteen-year-old would feel, when faced with an irate father after talking back to his mother."

Leroy nodded in understanding. "Been there. Done that. Not smart. So what is it that causes this?"

"I wish I knew. There is something so deep about it: just a real, primal fear. Maybe fear mixed with regret or sadness or … Hell, I don't know. It just really sucks. Bad enough to worry me about what's wrong with me." I didn't tell him about the third grade; some things are better forgotten.

There was silence for a few moments, and then Leroy suggested that I talk with Don and Jane about it.

"Les, I certainly felt fear a number of times, particularly at the beginning. Still, what you seem to be talking about is at a much deeper level than anything that I have experienced. Ask them. See what they say."

"Well, maybe, but I don't have the money. My insurance won't cover most types of counseling and I can't afford the rates they would charge."

"Oh! That's no problem. They do a lot of talking with students before or after class. Just hang around after class and ask them. Or call up first and set a time before or after class. They see this kind of thing as part of the class. They do it all the time. They talked with me a number of times."

"So what would I tell them?"

"Just what you've told me. They're good at what they do, so let them do it. They'll help you figure out where the fear is coming from."

It made sense, but I still couldn't see myself doing it. I didn't want to take advantage of them as counselors just because they had me in class. But probably, more truthfully, I wasn't sure at that point that I wanted them to know how much this was bothering me.

Or it could have been that the fact that it was bothering me was also bothering me … It didn't make sense to me. This system was one of the most rational and ethical martial arts systems of the three, that I had tried out. Still, it bothered me in ways that the other two hadn't. This just didn't make sense. I finally decided that I would put it off for a while, and if it didn't go away, I would revisit the question of talking with them.

five

Green Belt Sessions

One Attacker, Unarmed, Moving

"Our defenses are designed to work better mov-
ing than standing still—so let's get moving!"
—Jane

"At this level, the center of you and your attacker exists somewhere within
the outer reaches of the two of you. Find it, use it, or lose the fight."
—Don

FIRST TWO MONTHS

With those two quotes, our initiation into throws and holds began. The first one made sense and felt exciting. The second one was confusing and felt like gibberish at first. Then Don reached into a box and took out a piece of wood and a wine bottle and flipped the box upside down to make a table.

The three-inch wide wooden strip was beveled on one end and had a hole in the center at the other end. Don put the narrow end of the wine bottle through that hole and set the beveled end down on the box. The wooden strip and bottle were at a sharp angle and seemed unstable.

He adjusted the bottle inward just a little and this time both the wooden strip and the bottle stood together perfectly balanced in the air with just the bottom of the wooden strip touching the box.

I had seen this type of wine bottle holder before in stores, but never up close. Until now, I had only seen it as a cute novelty. Don pointed at the wooden holder. "This is you, defending or throwing; the bottle is your opponent. If the only thing you know is where your center of balance is, you will not be able to throw. If you also learn where their balance is, then you can throw, but only during practice. If you are going to throw or defend at all in the real world, you will have to know where the center is for both of you."

He took the bottle out and put the strip back on its beveled edge and, not surprisingly, it fell over. He then inserted the bottle again and stood them back up on the box. He repeated the phrase, this time with great emphasis.

"Without finding the center for the two of you, you won't be able to throw at all in the real world. This skill won't be learned overnight. Learning it will be a process. You will be finding your own center of balance more and more, and at the same time you are learning to find the balance point between the two of you. It's a process. Don't expect to learn it overnight.

"From this process you can learn one of the most valuable lessons we can teach you, and it applies to all of life: 'Give up the struggle for perfection. Aim instead for progress.' Success in anything you attempt or do is a case of being balanced and staying within reasonable parameters. It is not trying to hit that bull's-eye called perfection.

"Learn this lesson and you can learn to be content in your life. Miss this point and you will be condemned to a life of drivenness and obsession, insecurities and feelings of inferiority."

With that, our first lesson in throwing other people began. A friend of mine had studied a throwing art and he used to come back really beaten up from being used for throwing practice by some of the more advanced students. While that was probably an exception to the rule, I was a little nervous. Don motioned several advanced students to come over and work with us, and my nervousness increased.

My fears vanished when they began to throw us so that we could learn how to fall well, not so they could get in some practice. One of them told me that they use a different form for the hip throw when they're teaching someone to fall than when they're actually using it. They would wrap their arms around us and, grabbing our belt, lift us with their hip. Then, pulling us around their back, they'd gently place us on the mat and then correct our position. As we improved, they threw us a little quicker, but still held on to us in such a way that they could pull us up quickly if we were about to land in a way that could harm us. Over time, the throws got faster and harder, but everyone moved at his or her own speed.

Surprisingly, when it was time for us to learn how to throw, they were the ones who took the falls from certain throws. One of them explained that beginners often throw people badly. Some of the positions that beginners put people in could do real damage, so only advanced students were allowed to take the falls from beginners. They weren't allowed to take the falls until they had been trained how to get back into good positions to land. It was a point of pride to become good enough to take falls from beginners.

Our first throw we learned was called *kuchiki taioshi*, or dead tree drop. It was a leg throw, and while it seemed weird and I couldn't figure out how you would use it on the street, it did work very well. When you were thrown you went down like a dead tree. One moment you're standing up, and the next moment you're flat on your back. Hard. The second time I forgot to tuck my chin. My head snapped back and hit the mat. Thank God for those two inches of foam. As it was, the room spun for a while, and I had a headache that lasted into the next day.

Once we had the principle down, they showed us how to apply this throw. We didn't use it the first way we learned. Instead, they showed us how to get into it from a number of positions or situations. It was amazing the number of ways that it could be used. You could use it falling down, being shoved down, or being attacked with a chain or chair, and you could do it from in front, behind, or the side.

We couldn't practice it very fast on each other, as it would break the knee of the one being thrown, so they brought out a bag and we began to use that for full attack. Then they added how to roll over the opponents once they were down, using your elbows. It would pretty well end all resistance, if there was any left after their head had hit the ground.

I left class that night thinking about being a better fighter each time I left class. I had learned a number of basic techniques in Orange Belt, but now I could see what they had been saying: all of this worked better when everyone was moving. And it really did work! This throw was simple, practical, and really efficient. As I got out of the car at the school parking lot, I looked at the blacktop and thought about landing from this throw on that instead of a mat.

There it was. That sudden, sick feeling again. I reached out to the car to steady myself and then tried to calm my stomach down. I was breathing hard and had broken into a sweat. It took several minutes before I was somewhat sure that I wouldn't vomit right then.

Something was going on. It wasn't a simple feeling of nausea that came and went. This went much deeper and it stayed with me, sometimes for days. It was deeper than just awareness of the potential damage that throw could do. It was a sickness that went to the core of my being. Or maybe it came from my core. At that point, I just couldn't tell, but it didn't go away. It seemed to be getting worse over time.

This had happened maybe three or four times during Orange Belt, and I had come to dread this feeling. I began to wonder if there was something wrong physically that was being triggered by this, but deep down I knew that there was nothing wrong with my body. There was something in my soul—in the very depths of my being—that was having trouble with all of this.

I had to get a handle on this. It was now beginning to disrupt my life outside the Dojo, and I was already dreading having these times in the Dojo.

MIDDLE PERIOD

Green Belt was taking longer than I had hoped. There was just so much to learn. It wasn't that there were a huge number of techniques, but we had to learn so many basics. We had to learn to fall and throw. We had to learn to time our blocks and blows to the person's movements. We had to learn how to move their body out of balance while keeping our own. We began to explore our centers while learning where theirs were. We had to learn where the openings were, and they were always moving because we, and the person attacking us, were always moving.

Each time we mastered a section, such as falls or blows or kicks, we got another green stripe on our belt. By the time you had seven stripes you were a Green Belt. Don and Jane kept saying, "hang in there, Green Belt is halfway to Black."

It made sense. While there were three more ranks between this and Black Belt, none of them introduced so many basic concepts that had to be mastered.

Martial arts can be divided into systems that teach strikes and kicks, throws, and/or holds and locks. While most teach a lot of one and little of the others, our system taught them all equally and they all had to blend together seamlessly.

As frustrating as it was sometimes, there were several things that kept me coming back. One was the spirit of the place. It was fun as well as challenging. It was also, probably, the most positive point of the week for any of us. Mistakes were taken lightly and seen as positives, as learning points.

Once when I tried to throw someone with a new throw, I pivoted way too far around and wound up with this really heavy person stretched over my back and shoulders. I couldn't hold his weight up for long, but I couldn't throw him either, so I ended up in a heap under him. Don was down on one knee immediately, looking into my face and checking me out.

"Are you okay?"

"All but my ego."

"Well, if it's hurt too badly, I'll do a funeral service for it when it dies from its injuries."

The person I had tried to throw had rolled off of me by this time, and I had enough air in me to laugh. The whole place started laughing as I got up. That was the strange thing about this place: everyone was laughing at what happened, but there was no one who was actually laughing at me or making fun of me.

I felt better about myself after that inept attempt at something new than I had many times elsewhere when I had succeeded and was given a compliment. Maybe it was the fact that everyone here had had similar experiences and knew that they would have them again before too long. Most of it was this open atmosphere that Don and Jane created.

It was a safe place to learn, but not because just anything would be tolerated, and maybe that was part of the issue: There was no tolerance for carelessness; safety was paramount. And there was no tolerance for putting others down. The issue never came up, but sexual harassment never would have been allowed. There was so much intimate body contact, but it was done in such a way that no one ever felt fearful of being abused in any way. To be sure, there were some who were nervous or even frightened at first by being touched, but the safety of this Dojo helped them work through their issues.

The other reason it wasn't as hard to take the flop and the laughter was the way Don then corrected my form.

"I assume that you have figured out that something didn't work right," he said with a grin. "Do you need for me to help you with it, or do you have it?"

"I turned about forty-five degrees too far."

"You've got it. Try it slowly. Load, but don't throw a couple of times, then go to the throw. If you can load this one without throwing, then you've got it. The throw is ten times easier than just loading. Let me know if you need help."

It took a couple of times, but I got it right and then the throw went like a charm. It was the safest place to learn I had ever been. And yet, off and on, the fear and sense of dread that I had felt that first day kept coming back.

THE TEST

It was the end of five long months of work, but things were starting to pull together. Jenna and Leroy had moved on up in the ranks. She had gotten her Blue Belt and Leroy his Green Belt a month after my Orange Belt. Four months later, Jenna was going for Purple Belt and Leroy was just about ready for Blue.

By the time I had gotten my Green Belt, they had caught up and passed at least six or eight others who had started much earlier. While I'm sure that might have caused some feelings for the others, that was the way class was. You moved at your own pace and you were judged on how hard you worked and how far you had come, not how fast you moved up. Perseverance was highly valued.

I certainly wasn't at the level of the upper belts, but my moves were beginning to flow more smoothly and I was putting all of it together more naturally. Now, when someone grabbed me, I could move quickly and in a way that avoided the force of the attack.

When someone threw a blow or reached for me I could block, deflect, or gate-swing, whichever seemed to work. Once or twice things happened so fast that I wasn't aware of what I was doing until the move was over. It was a phenomenal feeling! It was like a moment of pure grace: as if everything I was all worked flawlessly at once. I was hooked.

The test was where it really came together for me. I demonstrated the moves. Strikes, kicks, punches, blocks, throws, falls … they all came together pretty well. They were becoming natural to me and it showed. But the final section, the self-protection part, was where my real breakthrough came. I had always done well at these, but that day I found myself. It was more than just being "on."

Something snapped, and the techniques blended quickly and naturally. I came to understand the phrases of "no-mind" and "moon reflecting on water" from within my body. They weren't phrases that I *sort of* understood: they were real. As I defended myself from attack after attack and everything fit together seamlessly, I could see things almost before they started and then respond without thinking.

The strangest learning though, was an awareness that came to me that morning in that few seconds between defenses. All the time that I had been at the Dojo, I realized that it had felt more like I was relearning or remembering something I already knew. It didn't feel like these were techniques that I was learning for the first time.

It was more like reaching back deep into the recesses of my mind and finding memories stored there a long time ago. Only I hadn't known these techniques before. Most of them I hadn't even seen. But I understood them at some deep level in my being. I had felt this all along during the time at the Dojo, but hadn't consciously been aware of it until that moment, a little over halfway through the defense section.

That day it had all come together, and with that I felt a power flowing into me. It filled me in a way unlike anything I had ever experienced before. I wasn't just fast; I was sure. I was certain in my moves. They were me and I was them. Being and doing were the same thing. I was doing what was right for me in that setting and I knew it.

It didn't matter what techniques I did, they flowed and they were right. And I did them with a certainty and an authority that was beyond my rank. They used the word "Warrior" a lot in class, and that day I claimed that as myself.

Lots of students talked of wanting to learn to be a Warrior, and I had wanted it too. But on that day, I came to know that all that time that

I had been at the Dojo, learning the techniques and attitudes and becoming aware of the world around me in new ways, I actually hadn't been learning to be a Warrior—I already was a Warrior. I was just learning the skills that were already mine.

I finished the test. Don reported my scores, telling me that most of my defense work was on Black Belt level. I was stunned and yet I wasn't. I knew that day, that on some level, I had jumped light years ahead.

six

Green Belt Sessions

Aftermath

As soon as they finished telling me about my test scores, I turned and looked around the room. Leroy was grinning openly. A number of students, some who had been there much longer than I, stared at me with a look of awe—one or two bordered on a touch of envy.

Jenna was smiling, but I could see a sense of puzzlement and confusion in her. She was looking at me as though she had just had some deep insight into me that she hadn't seen before.

I felt great.

Strangely though, it didn't feel even slightly like pride. It was a deep learning of self, a finding of something in me that I had not known to that point. Something else, something really deep.

And when it happens, that kind of knowledge precludes pride. It is more akin to peace, settling into your skin, or finding that place in the universe that was reserved for you. I just didn't have the words for it at that point in time. But I had changed, and I knew that I could never go back.

I turned back to Don and Jane as the class started to break up and head out. They were both smiling, but it was strange. They were looking at me very intently and smiling as though they were privy to some secret I hadn't been let in on. I didn't know what to say. Or ask. I couldn't even grasp what had happened.

Jane just quietly and very intensely said to me, "I told you, that first day you found your way to the Dojo. You belong here."

Don looked at me very seriously and said, "Next Sunday. That's when your real training will begin. We've seen that fear that is deep within you. It's kairos, Les. God's time: time to face it. There isn't an option; it doesn't matter whether you want to or not. It's time, and if you don't willingly turn and face it, the Universe will hunt you down and force the issue. Either way, it's time. Next Sunday the training starts in earnest."

There was something in his voice and the look on Jane's face as they stood there that set off that fear again, and I shivered deeply from my core. I felt my knees go weak and that all-too-familiar sick feeling took over. Only much worse: much, much worse.

Reality was swirling and I wasn't sure if I could catch myself this time before I lost control and could never get back. I knew that I was about to collapse straight down into a heap or fall over. Whichever happened, I wasn't going to have a say in the matter. I staggered back a step or two.

Jenna and Leroy had been hanging back slightly, while Don and Jane were talking to me. Jenna quickly stepped forward and put her arms around mine. "Are you okay?" I nodded numbly, too weak and too unsteady to lie out loud. Leroy took my right arm in his hand and, half supporting me, turned me and headed me toward the door.

A lot of the class had been crowding around behind them, waiting to talk with me, but they got one look at me and faded away. Probably didn't relish the idea of being around if I blew my cookies, which felt likely at that point.

"Man, you look like hell," Leroy said. "You need to call them up and set a time to talk. You hear me? You need to call them and set a time. You are flat going to have to get over this shit."

"Les? What's he talking about? Leroy, what shit? What's going on?" Jenna sounded puzzled, worried, and a little pissed at not knowing what was going on.

We had only had a couple of dates in March and April and really hadn't started dating seriously until the last of May, but then we had grown really close, really fast. Within a month we were planning our lives together, talking late into the night too many nights a week, and talking of marriage, although no proposal had been heard by either of us.

But I hadn't gotten around to telling her was about these periods of deep fear. I hadn't told her anything about the way they came on, what it was that triggered them, or the depression that would last for days afterward. At first I had been afraid to share them with her for fear of scaring her off. But then later I hadn't mentioned them because, unlike Leroy, she hadn't seen them, and I didn't know how to start explaining them.

I didn't even know what they were or how to describe them. But it was clear that now I had no choice; the time had come. Like it or not, I was going to have to try to explain it all to her now.

We had driven up in my car so I told them, "One of you will have to drive, but if you can get us to the Breakfast Shack, I'll buy. And," I said, looking at her, "I'll explain it there. I just need a few minutes to collect myself."

Leroy looked around me at Jenna and stated calmly, "Don't worry. He's fine. Other than being psycho and a little weird, he's okay."

"Oh, is that all it is?" She relaxed a little and let the breath she had been holding escape. "It's just that he's crazy? Hell! I already knew that. As long as it isn't something serious. Besides, I've never used 'normal' and 'Les' in the same sentence before, anyway."

"Thanks guys. I appreciate your support."

"No problem," Leroy said. "Happy to do so. After all, you offered to buy breakfast. That's assured my life-long friendship and undying support for at least the next hour or two."

Jenna drove and I rode shotgun. Leroy stretched his legs out on the back seat. We spent the first few minutes of the trip in silence. Jenna asked a couple of times if she was taking the curves too fast, but mostly there was silence. I had a lot of time to think.

I still had the sense of fear, coupled with doom and dread, but felt a little better because it was out now with Jenna. And Don and Jane apparently already knew. Still, it was really bugging me.

Several times I had had fleeting thoughts of dropping out of the Dojo, because it was here that this first happened and it had never happened except in connection with the Dojo. But today, I knew that there was no way that I could drop out. I had to keep coming. I had found myself—and a home.

And the idea of the Universe hunting me down was more that I wanted to think about, even though I had no idea what he was talking about. But still there were doubts that started to creep in. Maybe I should leave. Something was wrong—deeply wrong.

One of the main principles that we had learned in Green Belt was escape through an opening. They had told us that later on we would learn to find openings that weren't obvious, or even create openings that weren't there. But at this level, we just had to learn to see and use the ones that were there. I had grasped the concept early on, but it was hard to do. In a fight, both of you are moving and the openings keep changing.

Jane told us over and over that at first we would see the openings after they had closed and it was too late to use them. Then we would start to notice them and respond; at that stage it would work some of the time. The next stage of growth was to see them as they opened, and then your success rates would improve a lot. Eventually, you would see them before they started to open, and then, when they did, you would be already there, waiting and ready to use them as you chose.

That was what had happened during the test. I "saw" them before they occurred and took advantage of them. I found out what she had meant when she said that, when you get to this level, you would see them without seeing them, know them without thinking of them, and use them without knowing what you did. I wasn't where the upper-level Black Belts were, but now I knew what she meant.

This was not just a technique for Jujitsu; it was a way of doing life. The trouble was that I just couldn't see an opening in this problem with my fear, my disgust, my depression over what I was doing. What I was doing? Was that really what I was reacting to—what I was doing in the Dojo? Or was it something deeper? Slowly, I began to think that maybe it was worse than that. Maybe it wasn't what I was doing.

Maybe what I was reacting to what I was ... myself—ME! It wasn't what I was doing, but who I was. I was training to kill, and what's more, I was not only good at it: on some level, I knew that it was who I was.

I was someone who was born into the world with the destiny of hurting people.

That wasn't what I had wanted for myself. It was antithetical to everything I had learned about myself or wanted for myself. I had often thought that I would want to be good at defending myself and, someday, my family. I wanted to be powerful, but also kind, generous, and likeable. But not this, not some steely-eyed killer.

But damn it! Wasn't that what my brother and sisters used to say? That when I got mad my eyes would turn from soft blue to hard steel? It hit me that what I had been afraid of all those times in the Dojo was ... myself.

And that's what had happened that first Sunday at the Dojo, when I watched Don and Jane work out. I saw in them power, self-control, and a really deep commitment to a life-and-death process. It wasn't that I *wanted* to be like that; on some deeply hidden level I knew that I *was* that. I was a fighter, a Warrior ... but also a killer.

Oh God! What of Jenna? How could anyone love someone with that type of mentality? How could someone love a person who had that emotional neutrality about death in the midst of a fight? That's what it was that I felt today during the test: I was doing this with no emotion ... no fear and no remorse.

Just reacting to the situation: in one move, taking the attacker's arm off of my neck and breaking his arm ... avoiding a thrust to the eyes and taking out the attacker's throat ... gate-swinging out of the way as someone tried to choke me from the front and then using my elbow to smash his face ... going down with a tackle and then breaking the attacker's neck while rolling ...

I was a person with no soul, someone who could kill with no emotion! How could Jenna live with me? How could *I* live with me?

Deep down, the first time I saw Don and Jane work out, I had known it. I had known that I could fight and kill without feeling. And that was what had been eating at me from that point on.

Today I had not only demonstrated my skill, I had demonstrated my ability to remove myself from the presence of death, to calmly accept the possibility of my mortality in the fight, and then to go on to do whatever damage I needed to inflict. This was not the "me" that I had wanted to become. I hadn't come here for that ... or had I?

Oh, shit! Maybe I had. Maybe I had come for just that reason. Maybe I had sensed their presence and had led myself to the Dojo so I could perfect the killing. I felt panic and nausea rising together.

Slumped in the seat, I turned and pressed my face against the window, and the tears ran down my face. I slowly became aware that all this time in the Dojo, during all those periods of fear and depression, I had been trying to come to grips with the monster I was inside. And there was no opening to escape through on this one. You can unload a gun, but I had already loaded myself, and there was no unloading of that.

It was done.

Before I knew what I had done, I had loaded myself to kill and that could never change. My course was set. I had become a version of myself that I hadn't known existed, one that was far from what I had dreamed of becoming.

And then the sobs came. Slowly and quietly at first, but then my body heaved over and over. I rolled down the window, gulping, needing to devour some fresh air. But it was the hot July air that hit me, and I knew I couldn't last much longer. Jenna must have sensed what was happening, because she whipped the car over to the side and skidded to a stop, throwing gravel everywhere.

I got out just in time and held onto the car so I wouldn't lose my balance and fall into the mess I was spewing onto the shoulder. I just stood and shook, puking all the while. Then I sobbed, and then hurled some more. Finally, I settled down. Jenna wiped my forehead with some cool water she had poured on her hand from a bottle. I realized Leroy had been holding me steady for some time.

Eventually, we got back into the car. The air conditioning felt so good on my skin that I let myself go into it. I must have dozed, because when I woke up we had come to a stop by Leroy's house.

"What about the Breakfast Shack?"

"Jenna's taking you home. I'm going to get my car and join you all there. I'll pick up something for us to eat. Anything special that you want?"

"Fries. A big platter of cheese fries."

"You got to be kidding. After what your stomach just went through, you're going to shovel it full of cheese fries?

I nodded.

"Okay – cheese fries it is. Jenna?"

I only remember the rest of the day in snatches. Somehow we had gotten into the house. Leroy brought something for lunch. Then, snuggled on the couch between the girl that I loved and my friend, we worked our way through the story of the fear and my new insight.

It was dark out when Leroy left. He turned and said very firmly, "Call them. Damn, man, you cannot go on like this. You don't call them, I will. Friends don't let friends drive drunk and friends don't let friends live like this, either. Call them. Tomorrow. Or I do."

I woke up just as the sun rose and found myself in bed, wrapped in Jenna's arms. She knew. Now, she knew.

And she hadn't left.

Oh my God! She hadn't left.

I had no idea why, but she hadn't left. She was still there!

seven

Interim

"But a weak man with his back to the wall can be more dangerous than a strong one. The strong one knows he can probably save himself to fight another day, but the weak one suspects that he can't."
—Melancholy Virgin, Anabel Lee.

Jenna was in the shower when I called out to the Dojo. Jane answered and listened to my scrambled explanation of what happened. I found myself getting sick again and just stopped.

"Its okay, Les. You looked awful when you left. We've watched you since that first day. You're fighting a terrible battle inside.

"Are you working today? No? Okay, come on out around 12:30. We'll have lunch and talk. Jenna and Leroy are welcome too, if they're free."

"Okay." I hung up.

Just after I set the phone down it hit me that I hadn't even been polite. No "Thank you," no "Goodbye." Just hung up. Downright rude, but I didn't have the energy to call back. I'd apologize when I got there, but in the meantime, they would just have to understand.

"Who was that on the phone?"

"We're going to the Dojo for lunch."

"Good thing I'd decided not to go to class anyway."

"Oh—Sorry. I'm just …"

"It's okay. That'll be good. You need to talk with them. Where do we meet them?"

"I dunno."

Jenna called back to find out if we were to go to the Dojo, their house, or the office. I was still too numb to realize that we probably wouldn't eat at the Dojo, which was the only place out there where I had been. I don't remember the rest of the morning or the drive out.

I do remember that we got to their house before I was ready. Oddly enough, one of the few other things that I remember was being struck by the thickness of the walls and that the door was recessed into them. I don't remember much else about the house except that a deep sense of peace hit me as we passed through the entry room and into the living space. Don and Jane were fixing lunch and Jenna pitched in to help. I sat on a stool by the breakfast bar and stared out the huge windows on the opposite side of the great room. The windows overlooked a wide porch and beyond in the distance, range after range of the mountains. I don't remember starting to eat or what we ate, but somewhere during lunch, Don and Jane began to talk with me and ask me questions about what was going on. My memory cuts back in with us sitting on the couch in their library, talking, and Jenna holding my hand in her lap with both of hers. I must have been starting to feel better, because what was being said was coming into focus.

Later Jenna told me that she had explained what had happened the remainder of Sunday after my test. Apparently Don and Jane asked me some questions that I answered, but I really don't remember anything except that the panic began to subside.

At some point Don was saying to me that part of what I was feeling was normal fear, part of it was an overreaction of my amygdala—I've forgotten what he said that was—and part of it was that I was more aware than most of the class of what a Warrior faced.

"Most of the students, Les, take a long time to even begin to experience, let alone understand, what you already are feeling. Warriors are not people who train so they can damage others, or people who on some level want to kill, or people who are full of rage or anger.

They are not people who can face death, never flinch, and not even care that someone has been hurt.

"Warriors are people who do care. And only those who care get hurt by what they do or may have to do. The ones who don't care aren't Warriors, they are just fighters." Don was looking out the window and yet seemed totally present with us.

"Warriors were created to walk through life with a terrible tension. They want peace. They dislike conflict. They never wanted to be born to their calling, but they were. This causes stress because they hurt for both the victim and the abuser. They are called to stand on the boundary line between the victim and the oppressor. Fighting, or at least preparing to fight, is their destiny, not their desire. And they are good at it. But to stay sane, they have to find a balance."

I could hear the pulse in my ears and I was tearing up, wondering if that could ever be said of me, hoping, yet … I started when Jane spoke.

"Yesterday, you came into full awareness of who you are. You moved through the Green Belt test like a Black Belt many years over. What came over you was not a fear of what you can do; it was the fear that comes with the sudden realization of who you are and what you have been called to do that set off this reaction yesterday. The little fear reactions that you have been having since you came to the Dojo have been leading up to this. Les, I know that you are going to want to turn and run from this, but where would you go? Wherever you go, you will still be there. However you may try to deny who you are, you will still be the same person at the core. It is not only okay to be a Warrior, it's good to be one. God created you this way, a Warrior."

She paused and gave this time to sink in before continuing. "The reason we spend so much time training people in our class is that it takes more time to train someone not to have to do damage than it does to kill. We could train effective killers in a period of months.

"Still, this new way of being doesn't feel good at first. It's kinda like being a teenager all over again. The problem with teens is that their knowledge far exceeds their life experience. Those of us who are farther down the path understand what you can't see now. It is good to be able to protect. Someone has to do it and those who just want to fight can't do so. They will become as the oppressor, fighting for the wrong reasons: fighting out of anger or rage, bringing harm to others, and damaging their souls.

"You are blessed with a rare talent and skill. You are also blessed—and cursed—with a deep love of people and a desire to bring beauty and good into the world, not harm."

Don then drew a deep breath and slowly let it out. "Les. The only way to conquer your fear is to push through it. To do otherwise is to court disaster. If you try to run from yourself due to fear of whom you think you are or what you think you might do, you could easily lose yourself and spend a long time in a very dark night of the soul. Better to struggle and deal with it now.

"The next rank is Blue Belt. You will learn to defend against weapons. It is in this belt more than any other that you will come to face yourself. You will find out how fragile life is, how quickly you could die, how you might have to kill even when you don't want to. In short, you will learn that life and death are the same thing. You can't live if you don't live daily with death—yours and others."

He paused and looked deep inside himself. "We just don't know about our death and its timing. Today I'm alive. One minute from now my life could be gone. Heart attack, stroke, aneurism … Or I could be here and Jane could be gone. So I appreciate the memories and cherish them now, before she leaves or before I go. And we live well today so that the last memories will be good ones. We live so that in the end, the story of our life will be a good one, worthy of the telling."

He relaxed back into his chair, while I continued to sit on the edge of mine. "Come to class next Sunday. Learn the defenses. Learn. Learn to defend against the gun or a knife. Learn to die. Learn to kill when there is no other way. Learn how not to kill, if possible. But learn. Learn what you were born to learn.

"Les, look at Jane. No—don't just glance at her. Look at her."

I did, but wasn't sure what I was to see.

"Are you afraid of her? Does she seem like someone whom children would run from? The truth is that children are always coming to her in restaurants and malls. And to me. They're not afraid, because we are not monsters. We are kind people who love children, teenagers, and adults. We just plain love folks."

"But you are Warriors," I interjected, still not sure of myself about this.

"*And* we are Warriors," Don corrected. "We are deadly, but we are not dangerous. In fact, we are safer than most people.

"Take the average person—one who has not had his nose broken or been knocked silly in a fight and still gone on, someone who hasn't trained for that. Let that person get hurt, and they could suddenly find a fear rising in them that they couldn't stop. Deep in their brain, a switch would be thrown and they could respond in a way that was out of control. They come to a few moments later holding the throat of someone who no longer is breathing, and they have no memory of how it happened.

"Far better to be one who is prepared, who can turn off the fear, keep emotions at a minimum, make a good decision, and then act with an appropriate level of response. One who will do little or no harm if possible, but kill only because there is no other way.

"That is what we are training you to do. It is who you are. You are a Warrior and you were born to protect those around you. Even if it never happens that you know of, just your presence will make the difference. Your being in the world may turn away evil, because you were there at the right time and the right place."

Leaning forward with hands folded, knees on his elbows, and looking straight into my eyes without blinking, he said quietly, "Les, what if you don't study anymore, someone attacks you, and you have to kill the attacker? Could you get up in the morning and look in the mirror and say, 'I gave my best'? Could you live with yourself if you hadn't prepared?

"Better to be good at these skills. Better to be the best that you can be and then, should you have to kill, you will be able to look in the mirror and know that there was no choice. They brought death into the situation, not you.

"It would still be hard, but you would know you did your best. And with that knowledge you could get over it in time and move on with your life.

"This Sunday, Les. Come. Don't walk away now. You'll regret it the rest of your life."

And with that it was over. Don leaned back, Jane got up and stretched. Jenna and I carried our glasses out to the kitchen. We both made a bathroom stop, said our thank you's, and then left.

We rode in silence for a while. Halfway down the mountain, Jenna asked me quietly, "Where are you? You okay?"

"I don't know. I'm a lot better than I was. At least I'm out of the fog I disappeared into. I don't think I've sunk that low in a long time. I don't even know if I was there. But I'm better now. Stay with me tonight. Please. I mean, I'll be all right if you can't, but I'm going to need to talk some and work this through."

eight

Blue Belt

One Person, Armed

"When faced with a weapon, you must accept that you are already dead.
"Anything that happens after that—a cut on the arm, a powder-burn on the
hand, or a bullet in the leg—is an improvement over 'dead'. Once you can
grasp that idea in the core of your being, you will be freed up to live."

—*Don*

Except for a nagging fear of what might happen when I returned to the Dojo, I began to feel more like myself as the week went by. By the time Sunday rolled around I was pretty much back to normal. There was a mixture of fear and excitement in me as we drove up the mountain, a mixture that kept building up as the emotions tumbled over each other. I was walking across the meadow toward the Dojo when the confusion peaked. It was really strange, though: the moment I stepped into the Dojo, the fear disappeared. Completely. And I was back to knowing myself.

Warmups went great, and then Jane took the advanced students to the mats for work, as it was a practice Sunday. One of the Black Belts took the beginners and Don called several of us over to the side and began our introduction into Blue Belt.

"Weapons are deadly. To be sure, someone could attack you bare-handed and kill you. The difference with a weapon, however, is that you know that anyone with a weapon wants to kill you, and that the weapon cuts your margin of error to almost zero.

"You can miss slightly in a block against a fist and pick up a blow to the cheek. Your head will react and you'll get out of the way before it can do too much damage.

"But if they were thrusting with a knife, you could lose an eye or take a bad cut. With a fist they will hit fully committed and the fist will continue on its way. With a knife, they rarely commit completely, so they can shift directions in mid-strike. Suddenly, the knife that has just cut your face will be slashing downward into your throat, the side of your neck, or deep into your shoulder. The first two options would kill you. If it cuts that muscle on the top of your shoulder, that arm will hang, shock will hit, and the odds have now gone much higher against you. Unless you get really lucky or they do something really stupid, they can play with you. Death will be slower.

"Except for situations like drunks who can barely stand up and are just annoying, you should start any fight, whether the assailant is armed or not, by assuming that it is a deadly attack, and then step the response down as quickly as you can. With weapons you must not only assume that it is a deadly attack, but step down the response only after you are completely certain that the assailant is no longer a threat.

"For example, say a person with a club attacks, and you do a block-parry-strike combination. The person flies away from you and you lose your grasp on him. He are standing there dazed. Not only can you not wait to see if it's over, you should have followed him so quickly that he wouldn't have had time to stand there. The moment the parry and strike knocked him away, you should have been following up with your next moves.

"Only when following him would put you in danger would you step back and get distance so you can regroup. Then when the timing is right, go back in to kill—even if he has been hurt and his attack is slower and far more shaky. Don't step your response down yet.

"Don't ever step your response down until the weapon is secured and the assailant is incapacitated. Notice that I didn't say 'dead' or 'severely injured.' That may be what it will take in some situations, but in some cases it could also mean that the person is gasping for breath because of a blow to the solar plexus, is lying stunned on the ground from a throw, or on a higher level of injury, lying on the ground with a broken elbow or non-functional knee. Then you check out the scene again. Are there other attackers, Friends coming to avenge the assailant? or are you clear? If you're clear, then you can step it down.

"Then you must go on the legal attack. Point at someone nearby and have them call the police. Tell them to say that someone was attacked by a person with a weapon, and that the attacker is on the ground. When the cops come, press charges. The one who files charges has the legal advantage. Don't give that up. It's a criminal case. Let the state pay for the attorney. Your fees to a private attorney to defend yourself in court will be high, and you will be trying to prove why you did this. Let the attacker be on that side of the argument.

"Now, let's talk weapons."

For the next fifteen minutes or so he talked about weapons defense theory in general as he showed specific examples. Then he moved to the basic groupings of weapons: bladed, firearms, stiff, and flexible. He said that we were going to have to learn to use all the groups on a basic level, as it was the only way we could understand how to defend against them.

From there he gave us the specific issues with each group and, using us for attackers, showed us the various difficulties in defending against each weapon. We started practice with only fifteen minutes left, which, though unusual for their way of teaching, still made sense. This was unlike anything we had studied before, and weapons posed huge variations in how we could get hurt.

We started with a club defense from a forehand, diagonally downward attack. That helped us get a sense of distance, timing, how to draw the attack when and where we wanted, and several totally different ways of approaching the problems when faced with a club.

At the end I stood with the rest of the class as always and recited the code of ethics, but this time it meant something even deeper. I began to understand it as more than just words. I suddenly realized that the code would have to be taken into the cells of my body, not just memorized, as there wouldn't be time to think this through in most situations.

DO NOT CONFRONT WHERE RESOLUTION IS POSSIBLE.

DO NOT ATTACK WERE CONFRONTATION WILL WORK.

DO NOT BLOCK WHERE DEFLECTION WILL WORK.

DO NOT CAUSE PAIN WHERE CONFUSION
OR RESTRAINT WILL WORK.

CAUSE PAIN OVER INJURY,
AND MAIMING OVER KILLING.

DO ONLY WHAT HURT YOU MUST—
ANYTHING ELSE IS VIOLENT AND YOU WILL
HAVE BECOME AS THE ATTACKER.

DO NOT DO LESS THAN YOU MUST—YOU WILL
HAVE LEFT A VICTIM DEFENSELESS AND A VIOLENT
PERSON UNAWARE OF THE NEED FOR CHANGE.

As we bowed and ended class I suddenly realized that my fear had left. No more hesitancy. I felt at home in my skin once more. I craved getting more information and couldn't wait for next week's practice. I was back in the groove and I was my old self. I was past the problem.

The three of us piled into the car, laughing at Leroy's running commentary on unwanted adventures in the vomit-mobile. I was so high from the workout I was giddy, and it became hard to breathe from all the laughing. I had to pull over and stop so I could catch my breath. It felt so good to be past such a low period as last week. I was still laughing as I pulled back onto the road. I didn't want to ever come down from this high.

"Breakfast Shack and it's on me. And this time, we *will* make it."

After several quick turns around sharp curves, Leroy started groaning in the back seat and pleaded for someone else to drive, saying that I had too much adrenaline in me. At the speed I was taking the curves he didn't think any of us were going to make it. "Even if we do," he said, "you keep this up and I'll have to get out and vomit. It'd serve you right. You'd get to hold me up while *I* puked."

"No problem," I responded as I slowed way down. "Look who's ahead of us."

There were loud groans in answer. It was Harriet. Harriet was a gutsy lady and everyone liked her, but no one wanted to get behind her coming down the mountain. Her car accident had damaged not only her hips, but also her sense of automotive adventure. She drove an adaptive van with hand controls—slowly. Very slowly.

"Great. A moment ago I thought I was going to either die or puke. Now, I'm facing starvation before I can even get off the mountain."

Somehow, Leroy survived it all.

MIDDLE WEEKS

Within about five weeks we had covered all the basic weapons defenses. Each week my time at the Dojo got better and better. After that first week, there had been no more fear as we approached the Dojo, just joy and excitement. Actually, there were no more periods of fear at any time during the workouts or the intervening weeks, but rather a deep joy that came from connecting in one perfect moment every now and then, even if just for a second. I knew who I was and where I was headed. I was where I belonged.

Things at work were going great too, and I was getting lots of kudos there. The company I worked for designed and manufactured pneumatic pumps for industry. As a mechanical engineer, I was on the design side. Some of the pumps were small; some were so large that the parts had to be handled with a hoist and the finished project would need a crane for loading onto and off a truck.

I wasn't far enough along to design a whole pump or do the reviews of other engineers' designs. I just did one or two parts of it, but a couple of times lately I had been given an entire section. At my one- and three-month evals, my boss, Larry Hartfield, had told me I was doing better than any new hire he had managed. They had great hopes for me.

However, Sundays at the Dojo were different. Work was about what I *did*: ideas, projects, building pumps with other designers, working with suppliers and contractors.

The Dojo wasn't just about what I did; it was also about me—about who I *was*. There in the Dojo, who I was and what I did were the same. Doing and being—one thing. Even when I had trouble with some of the techniques, it was still about one thing. I was learning about me and being me. I was what Don and Jane called a "human becoming."

Leroy had been working with some white belts on their *atemi* (striking techniques). He was not able to make class this Sunday, so Don asked me to cover for him. They were doing okay, but didn't have much force behind their blows. I worked with them on form and speed on a heavy bag in order to help them develop more power. Their problem didn't seem to be in hitting the bag, but in their understanding of the blows themselves. I decided I needed to explain to them a little better. I motioned them to the side of the mat.

"Come on over to the side and sit down. You are all punching okay, but not nearly powerfully enough. You are hitting too softly and I think I know why: You think that you are supposed to hit the surface of the target, but you are supposed to be hitting through the target to the back of it. Remember the line from the bottom of the nose around the bottom of the ear and to the notch at the back of the head? Remember that lecture? Well, you are going to have to hit into the back of the head, not the front of it.

"You have to position your blow so that your arm doesn't fully extend until you've hit the back of the head. If you are hitting the stomach you must hit the spinal column before your blow stops. You can't hit one inch inside the stomach and think that will do."

I stood a student up and showed the proper distance for strikes and kicks moving to one side, so that they could see it in slow motion. I then cautioned him to stand still and did the same blow quickly and with power to the side. It would have driven his stomach up against his backbone. They got the idea.

"Hitting a throat? Do it fast and all the way through. Any structure in the attacker's body that is in the way needs to be pushed aside or flattened. Now, you all try it again."

They stood up and this time the blows began to look better. There was a commitment that they hadn't had before.

But I was dizzy. Reality was swirling again, only much faster, and there was not a tree to hold on to. That thought took me back to that first Sunday when I sat on these mats thinking, "At least this is safe. How far can you fall when you're sitting down?" That day I found out. Very far.

The swirling suddenly constricted into a vortex and pulled me in and I began to get sucked down. I don't remember if I sat down or my legs buckled under me, but suddenly I was on the mat. I felt a huge hole open up under me and the vortex dropped me through the mat and into a huge pit. I was falling fast, arms flailing, trying to find something to grab on to. Instead I just kept tumbling. It was like that dream where you fall and then wake up with a start before you hit … Only I kept falling and the pit was black and the sides too far apart to grab anything. I heard a scream coming from way down inside of myself.

I sensed a change and I realized that the rate of fall was slowing down. Though I was still falling I began settling out of the tumble and eventually moved slowly upright and into my seated meditation position. My hands moved from clawing desperately into a lotus pose: thumb and middle finger together. And I settled onto—well, nothing. I was just suspended and sitting.

I heard Jane's voice inside my head saying, "Breathe.

"Deeply.

"Breathe in.

"Hold it.

"Breathe out slowly."

Again and again, until I had moved to some deep place of calm. For a moment, when I first realized that I wasn't sitting on anything but air, I am sure I started to descend again, but her voice caught me and brought me to a halt. We breathed in and out together. Slowly. Over and over. And then I realized that in this reality, sitting on air was perfectly normal.

And that was when I began to rise. I floated lightly up and was back to the top of the pit in just a few seconds. The rising felt slower than the fall, but seemed to take much less time than the falling. That didn't make sense either.

And then, very gently, I was back. The mat closed up under me and I was sitting on it. I breathed in and out a few more times and opened my eyes. Jane was there, sitting in the same posture that I was. The tears started to overflow my eyes and she reached out and touched my cheek.

"It's okay, Les. You're safe. You just saw a shadow side of yourself and it caused you to spin out of control. It didn't feel good, but it's not supposed to. What is important is that you found it. And you found it here, not out in the world somewhere, where it might have showed up uncontrolled.

"You're back now. Practice is over for you today. Just go sit quietly and meditate. Whatever thoughts come in, welcome them and don't try to push them away or to analyze them. Just do what happens. We'll talk after class for a few minutes."

I didn't realize that Don was off to one side until I heard his voice. "Jane, why don't you sit with him? I'll pick up the class."

I looked around and everyone was trying to go on as though nothing had happened, but the mood was different—way different. I wondered if the scream had come from my mouth or was only in my mind. I didn't voice the question because I was in no shape to find out. I got up slowly, wobbled over to the side, and tried to meditate for the last thirty minutes. I joined class for the final closing and was trying to sneak out the door to go home when Jane caught me by the arm and asked to see me off to the side.

"Les, we've noticed that a lot of times in class, you seem to struggle really hard with the consequences of having to hurt someone. Are you okay? Some struggle is normal, but there seems to be something much deeper going on with you."

"I'm okay. It's just that—I mean—Well, it's hard to explain. You see, once when I was a kid … Never mind. It really isn't that important."

I shifted my eyes around, trying to avoid eye contact with her, but I knew that Jane was staring at me. When I looked up I saw her looking intently into my face. She locked eyes with me and quietly said, "Les, you need to come see us. I don't know what happened, but we need to get to the bottom of this. There's no point in anyone carrying this kind of pain, this kind of worry, this kind of fear. You need to get it out and move on."

I nodded, told her I would call, and then made my escape along with Jenna and Leroy.

We all drove home in silence. Jenna and Leroy exchanged glances a couple of times and I would have given anything to know what they were thinking, but I never found the energy to ask.

nine

The Pit

One Person, Exposed to Himself

I didn't have to be forced this time. I called shortly after I got home and set up an appointment for right after work. I don't remember work, but I do remember going into their house, and while I was in the process of sitting down, I blurted out the question that had been haunting me.

"Am I going crazy? Is this a psychotic break?"

"No. You're not going crazy; you're going sane," Don said. "And it wasn't a psychotic break. It was a view of reality that most people can't see."

"Isn't that the definition of crazy?"

"Could be—for someone who can only see with their eyes. But just because someone else is blind, don't let them convince you that you are psychotic because you can see what they can't."

Jane chimed in. "Les, there are huge differences between mystics and psychotics. Some mystical experiences are very frightening and may require some period of time to grow from. Mystical journeys are not safe and secure ones. They are often dangerous, and people can lose themselves to psychosis along the way.

"There are some general guidelines, however. Mystic experiences leave the person grounded, whereas psychotic experiences leave them scattered or fragmented, long-term.

"Mystical experiences leave a person with a balance between a deep sense of self-worth and a deep sense of humility. Psychosis leaves one with a sense of superiority and delusions of grandeur.

"Mystical experiences give one a sense of purpose, allowing the recipient to give back to the world. Psychosis leaves the person with a sense of deserving to be served and needing support and care. There is a sense of being one with all of reality that leaves the mystic in a state of calm. Psychotics feel threatened and as if they are the only ones of worth.

"You have had a profound spiritual experience. You have journeyed into the depths of yourself and confronted the dark side of your nature. We will talk more later about the difference between the light and dark sides of spirituality, but that isn't what you think it is. Let's just say for right now that your dark side is also your salvation and the gift that you can give back to the world."

I felt lighter and my breathing had slowed and gotten deeper, but there was still a small knot in my stomach.

"We have known it from the first day you came to us," Jane went on. "The way you got there, your following of your instincts, your immediate commitment to this path, and your sensitivity to the vortex that was there, even when you first came here. You are not just a Warrior, Les. You are a Warrior-Priest. You have begun what some would call a shamanic journey. Others would call it a wilderness experience or a dark night of the soul. Whatever you call it, the truth is that you are being called.

"You are being called to go beyond simple learnings. Rather, you are going out to search deeply into your own soul and find all that is there. You are struggling with the issues of power and control. You are exploring the dark side of yourself. This is a good thing. That way you can find it before it finds you, overwhelms you, and causes harm to you and others.

"Les, can you name the battle going on within you? Sometimes naming or identifying the forces helps make it clearer."

I had thought about it, but I hadn't been able to put it into words, let alone name it. "It's sorta like … I look at the world, and when I see hatred and anger, I wonder if love isn't a more powerful force. I mean, if someone intent on doing harm came face to face with someone who was truly filled with love, couldn't that change them? Wouldn't that be enough? Even if the person wasn't changed immediately, wouldn't it in the long run make a big enough difference?

"I've been thinking … what if someone was about to shoot me and I took the gun away without hurting them, but then just gave it back? What if I just looked deeply into them and let them see the love I had for them? What if I told them that they might not understand why I was willing to do this, but they could go ahead and kill me?

"What if I just stood there and, while they were doing it, told them that I loved them and forgave them? Wouldn't that make a difference? I mean, every morning when they got up and looked in a mirror, wouldn't they see my face looking back at them?

"And wouldn't they ultimately come to see the strength that I had because of a love that they didn't have? Wouldn't that make a difference? Isn't that how Gandhi changed the course of history?"

They didn't say anything for a while, but just sat quietly. Then Don asked, "So have you read Gandhi?"

"Well, no, but I've read a lot about him."

"Not the same thing and somewhat dangerous in this case."

"So that is what hit you today," he commented. "Okay, you've named the surface level struggle, but what was the trigger?"

Jane continued the thought for him. "I was listening to the talk you were giving the class, and in teaching them to hit well, something you said or did triggered emotions from deep inside of you. What was it? Do you know? Can you put a voice to it?"

I sat there and once again the tears just started to flow. I didn't even know that they were that close to the surface. I didn't know what it was that triggered it and then suddenly I felt the vortex. And I was pulled back into that hole and I was falling down that pit again.

Only this time I realized that the hole wasn't around me; it was inside me. It never had been outside me. It had always been inside. I was falling deep into myself and I was headed for destruction if I couldn't work this out. I was falling into the pit of my fear. And then I saw the bottom.

Oh God! I saw the bottom! I could hear that scream again, a long way away.

The bottom was still far away but I could see it clearly. It was like a movie screen that showed my face as I talked to the students and talked of smashing through or pushing aside structures to make the blow work. And I saw my face attached to my soul and my soul was black, and I realized why the hole had opened up.

It wasn't that I was good at martial arts, or even that I enjoyed them. The pit opened up because at my very core I enjoyed the idea of hurting and being able to kill.

I had felt so good when I had been teaching them to smash through the body. I had enjoyed it! I was worse than a killer; I was a killer who enjoyed what he did. That's what all those times of sickness and swirling reality had been. I was finally seeing myself for who I was. I had been kidding myself my whole life. I wasn't a gentle kind of a guy.

At my core I was someone who not only could kill, but wanted to kill. I thought of all the damage that I was destined to do in the future and found that sick feeling coming over me. I couldn't allow it. I couldn't allow myself to become this.

I was falling faster and faster, and suddenly I knew that there was only one course I could take. I had to accept the fall and let myself hurtle down to the bottom of the pit and die there. I stopped flailing and focused on the bottom, willing myself toward that death before I hurt someone else.

I willed myself to turn head down and streamlined my body with my hands by my sides. I felt the speed pick up as I streaked toward the bottom. I braced for that awful collision and could already taste the metallic flavor that comes from getting hit on the nose or the head, but willed myself on. I was streaming downward and was waiting for the shock.

All of a sudden I was pulled sideways and there was a sudden jolt, but it was on my butt—and then another hard one on my back. I jolted out through the side of the pit and was slammed hard, right back into the realty I had started from. I hadn't hit the bottom.

I was supposed to be dead, but instead I was alive and sitting on their living room floor. I was confused and disappointed. Don was standing behind me and Jane was in front, holding onto my feet.

I didn't get it. The pit had been so real while I had been in it that this reality hadn't existed. Yet, now that I was back here, I could recall everything that happened here in detail. Almost as if I had been watching it from outside myself.

I had been sitting on the sofa, turning pale, going deeper into myself, hurtling downward, and just as I put my arms next to my body, Jane suddenly jumped forward, gabbed my legs at the ankles, and jerked me off the sofa and onto the floor. My butt hit hard. At the same time Don had stepped over the coffee table and as soon as I hit the floor he hit me on the middle of my spinal cord with the heel of his hand—hit me hard. The two jolts had brought me back to here and out of the pit.

I was overcome by disappointment. I had wanted to die. I had wanted this struggle to end. I had wanted to make the world safe from the terrible part of me that I had kept hidden from myself up to this time. But now I was back. I looked at them and began to sob. "Why? Why wouldn't you let me die?"

"Because we're Warrior-Priests and you aren't far enough along in this journey for us to let you make that decision. When you are far enough along, if you still want to die, then you can. Right now we had to stop that." Jane was sitting beside me, holding me and rocking. Don was doing some kind of pressure point massage on my head and neck, and I slowly calmed down.

A question popped into my head. "Could I actually have died by letting myself hit the bottom?"

"Sure. In our Western view of medicine, nobody dies without a physical cause," Don said. "We think that something physical has to happen. We don't even put down 'old age' as a cause of death any more. Something else has to happen to us. Something has to interrupt and stop life. We think that death isn't natural, that it is an exception. The truth is that death is a normal part of life.

"Both the Warrior and the Priest know this. But the Warrior-Priest doesn't just know it—he has experienced it within his own life. He has lived through his death and come back more whole than he started.

"To die, all you have to do is to turn loose. That was what you were doing. Having seen your dark side, scared of who you thought you were and afraid that you are evil and harmful, you decided to kill yourself as a way of preventing yourself from harming the world."

Jane chimed in, "Les, you don't know all there is to know of yourself yet. Believe me. Believe us. An evil person wouldn't have been concerned by finding that out about themselves. He would have rejoiced in it. Promise us that you won't end this until you have learned to put this in perspective.

"You see, what you see as your destructive side is also your healing side. All of us, when we are first confronted with our demonic, evil, or dark side—whatever you want to call it—are overwhelmed by it. But don't act on that feeling until you have been fully confronted by your good side also."

There was something about the jolt back that made me dizzy, but in listening to them I decided that killing myself wasn't the answer, either. Then I thought about the jolt. "What did you do to me? I mean the jolt and the blow on the back? What were they about?"

Don laughed. "You have just come back from trying to sacrifice yourself for the betterment of the world and you ask technical questions. Okay. What metaphorical system do you want the answer in?"

"Jeez, I don't know. Tell me in whatever metaphor you think I could understand." I was feeling both dumb and numb at that moment.

"Well, psychologists would say you were decompensating and that we used an aversion technique to shock you back to reality. That's an okay answer, but it misses out on the fact that you were actually planning to die at the end of the fall and so you would have. They wouldn't have been able to see that in you.

"Martial artists would say that you had an emotional shock and that we used *kappo*—resuscitation techniques. A doctor might say that you suffered psychogenic shock that appeared to cause a laryngeal/pharyngeal constriction with an overstimulation of the vagus nerve. They would say that the blow stimulated your sympathetic nervous system and the accelerator nerve took over and sped up your heart.

"A shaman might say that you had gone on a journey to the underworld that you were unprepared for and might not have returned from; that other shamans came to you and helped you reclaim your soul. Or it could be said that you had made, and were carrying out, a Warrior's commitment to protect the world from evil, even if it caused your death. So if you are the cause of the evil, plunging to your own death would be better than standing by and letting evil loose.

"Any way you look at it, what you did was based on love for the world, on good motives. You just aren't ready to make that decision yet, because you don't know the whole picture. Just a small part of it."

"And the jolt you gave me?"

"Let's just say that we saw where you were headed and didn't want you to stay in that reality. You aren't safe there yet. So we reached into it and brought you back to this reality."

"So, that pit was—is—whatever … a real reality? It's not a delusion or a psychotic break?"

"Well, some psychologists or psychiatrists might not agree with us, but some of them are blind to everything that isn't in their little box. From our worldview? You're not crazy; you're actually very sane. What you experienced was not only real, it was essential for you experience in order for you to become the best version of yourself. I'm glad you're making the journey.

"Actually, being a Warrior-Priest, you don't have any choice. Just promise us that you won't make that decision again if you should journey without us around. No matter how scared you are of yourself, come back until you can find us. God didn't create you with these tremendous skills just for you to end your life before it really got started."

Jane looked, took my chin, and turned it toward her face, as if I were a misbehaving child. "Can you see the end of this path yet, Les? No? Well, God can.

"So who are you going to trust about this? The one who can't see beyond the present and doesn't understand all there is to know of that, or the One who can see all? Your choice."

I sat there trying to make sense of it in my soul.

"Go wash your face and I'll get you a glass of iced tea."

"Sweet tea?"

"I'm one of the GRITS, Les. 'Sweet-tea' is the only kind of iced tea I know."

"Grits?"

"Girl Raised In The South."

Don put his arm on my shoulder and led me toward the kitchen, then in a very exaggerated drawl said, "She sho' 'nough is, Les. Come on in and sit a spell. You look like you're feelin' a mite puny."

I was … So I did.

ten

Time Out

One Person, Divided

Monday night I had spent with Don, Jane and "the Pit," as I have come to call it.

Tuesday night I had filled in Jenna when she came over after class.

Wednesday morning I woke up with a strange sense of calm. I thought through all that had happened, and too much was happening too fast. It was time to slow it down. I decided to take a few weeks off from the Dojo. The more I thought about it, the more it seemed right. I would call Don and Jane and explain, or perhaps just let Jenna tell them when she went this coming Sunday.

I realized that the longer I had been there, the more I had moved through the world aware of who and what was around me. What concerned me was that I was rehearsing in my mind what I would do if this person or that attacked me, or what I would do if someone came out of this place or that. This was not only normal according to people at the Dojo, but was encouraged.

According to Don and Jane—and some of the other Black Belts had confirmed this—while this was always done on some level, it ceased to be done at a conscious level after a while. But what if this awareness was causing my emotional attacks? I also realized that I needed to take a break from this if I were to be able to balance out my life.

Armed with this new outlook, I set off for work. I was still aware of potential threats, but partway through the morning I thought of something totally different: What if we were just as aware of the love around us? What if I looked at people in a different way, a way that asked what I could do lovingly if they attacked? Instead of defending, how could I respond in love? Or if I were to respond defensively, how would I respond while exuding love, defend, and then let them have their way?

I decided that I had to commit to being 100 percent pacifistic for this several weeks. Then I could decide at that point whether or not I would return to the Dojo. It was then that a thought struck me: could it be that if I were this aware of love and not wanting to hurt, that I could prevent evil from occurring around me by just sending out love wherever I went? The thought was strange, but considering all of the mystical things that happened in the Dojo, why couldn't it happen this way? I began to focus deeply on love.

At work the next day, I took breaks and my lunch hour to meditate and focus on sending out love. That night I did the same for an hour. I started to get excited about the possibilities and felt that I was exploring something far beyond anything that I had considered before.

The next morning I woke up more relaxed and more certain of my new path. If this kept up, then I would have to seriously consider whether I should stay with what Don and Jane were teaching. Perhaps they were doing well for some people, but maybe my path was different and on a different level.

Maybe I was to change the world by *not* fighting. Maybe that was the calling I had been created for. Or maybe I could develop a martial arts system that never did any harm. Maybe that was why I had come to the Dojo: to learn the basics that I could then change.

I was to meet Jenna after work at the mall for a quick dinner and a movie. I got there about forty-five minutes before our meeting time, so I sat down to focus myself on loving those around me. I was off to one side of the mall where the buses ran. It was usually full of a lot of older folks who came during the day, and then about this time the demographic would switch over to the younger working set, families, and teenagers who hung out here.

I came out of my reverie to the sound of voices. Not loud voices or even harsh voices, but voices whose tones were loaded with veiled threats. I looked over toward the indoor seats near the doors and a number of older persons were huddled and looking down at the floor.

A group of teenagers, maybe in their late teens, were moving among them, "asking" for bus money or money for food. The tone was clearly that of threat. It was obvious that they were using their youth, their strength, and their numbers to intimidate.

I moved toward them to defend the older people if needed. First, I stepped into one of the small shops and asked the worker behind the counter to call mall security, which was made up of off-duty cops.

When I realized what I was doing, I made myself stop and calm down. I thought of loving these kids, and then moved over toward them. I just stood behind them, projecting love, and eventually one of them noticed and the leader turned to face me. I smiled and asked, "Can I help you?"

"Yeah. We need money. Bus money."

At a couple of bucks apiece that would take most of the movie money, but that seemed a good trade. Money for peace. "That would be about $14. Here's $15. You have what you need, so I hope you have a nice ride and a nice evening."

"How much more you got?"

"You have what you need. Why would you want more?

"Because we ride the bus more than one day, jerk-off."

I was starting to shake in my faith as to whether love could work in this situation or not, but I tried to stay steady in my resolve to end this peacefully. I tried to look at them with a deep love for people that hadn't had all of the opportunities that I had. "One day at a time, my friend. This will get you home."

The leader glanced at his group. There was a bad look between them and I realized that my intervention had actually upped their level of nastiness to something close to hatred. Something wasn't working right; it should have been the reverse. Sensing love should have calmed them, not riled them.

I thought they were going to move toward me and tried to focus my resolve to not fight, to take the beating, moving just enough to avoid getting hurt badly. Then they just turned and were walking off.

I let out a sigh of relief and was starting to congratulate myself, thinking that maybe the kindness had produced too much strain for them to stay around, when I heard footsteps and a voice call out, "Police. Stay right there. We want a word with you." They had been getting ready to make a run for it, but three officers came around the corner from the other side and they were trapped.

The officers moved them to the side and began talking with them. I went quietly on by toward the main part of the mall and heard one officer question the leader as to where he had gotten the money that was in his hand. One of the senior citizens said, "That man gave it to them to bribe them to leave us alone." His friend said no, that he thought I was just buying time until the cops got there.

I wound up talking with the officers, trying to convince them that I had given the money to the teens freely and not because of threat. They were finally satisfied, and the sergeant came over and said, "I understand you were trying to be nice, but all you have succeeded in doing is convincing them that this works. Next time just call us, and then get out of the way."

I left upset, embarrassed, and confused. Jenna showed up in the middle of my talking with the police. I thought things were bad up to this point, but in explaining it to her, she just looked at me and said, "Oh, Les. Please don't let this pacifism struggle get you killed. I don't get what's happening to you. This really does seem crazy to me—more so than the Pit."

I suggested going to the movie before dinner; I'd put it on credit, and at least she couldn't see my blushing face in the dark. I would have time to think over what had gone on. I don't remember either the movie or my thoughts, but my feelings were very confused. Had I been wrong? Had I not been committed enough? If it had gone down to a fight and I controlled it but let them do their thing to a point, would that have changed things?

Or was I just being naïve or stupid? Still, I couldn't believe that what Gandhi had managed to do wouldn't also work for me, at least eventually. That raised the question of what Don had meant when he said there was a lot of difference between reading Gandhi and reading about him, and that it could be deadly. So what was the difference? I decided to find out. I also decided to continue on my present course. But I was pretty shook.

Still, I was calmer than I had been before. And I had stopped some without having to fight. Jenna and I walked the mall down to the food court, and I tried to explain what I was thinking. She listened. I couldn't get a read on her.

She sure was serious at first, but then she grinned. "Maybe, it wasn't as much about pacifism as it was about jujitsu. We are trained not to fight unless there is no other choice, you know. Maybe what you really did was find an escape through an opening. Isn't that in the Code of Ethics? 'Do not cause pain where confusion or restraint will work.' You called the police and then stalled. And paying $15 for the chance not to fight seems reasonable."

Shit. I'd just had a huge hole knocked in my philosophy. I'd never thought about "not fighting" as a strategy of fighting. So maybe pacifism could be a complete extreme of Waboku Jujitsu. That didn't make sense either, so I just quit thinking about it for the night. I was so tired and just wanted to go home.

Jenna insisted on following me home in her car and then going on. She laughed and said, "Hey, a girl needs to make sure her guy is okay, in case he gets attacked while he has a case of the dumbs."

I didn't see the humor, and told her so. She just looked at me and shrugged. "Too bad. You're getting seriously freaky, but I just hope you work your way out of this before it gets too bad."

Two days later, I was just as confused, but still feeling that I couldn't go on the way I was. I knew how good the Dojo had been for me, but then there was the issue of what I had seen in the Pit. I couldn't afford to make myself any more dangerous until I worked this out. I decided to drop the Dojo for a few weeks. I saw Don and Jane several times during this timeout, and while their insights helped, I couldn't get out of my mind what I had felt.

I had come to realize that it was something so primal that it scared me. I had mentioned this during a class back in Orange Belt, and Don smiled and looked a little amused. "Well, yeah. Fighting for survival is the most primitive urge we have, even before sex and mystical experiences. If you don't survive the attack by the lion you won't get to have sex, and your meditation times will be cut drastically short. That's why we train you so hard. Don't forget that it's easier to harm than not to.

"All the way along we have been working to help you survive and also to not hurt. That's what Brown Belt is about: to defend without hurting the other. Not always possible and sometimes it is entirely impossible.

Still, it is a worthy goal. If you stop now, you stop before you reach your goal.

"You will have stopped while primed to hurt, without being skilled enough not to. Stay with it until you are finely tuned. Then if things get out of hand and you hurt someone, you can at least look in the mirror and know that you did your best."

I committed to take one month off and see if I could get a handle on myself. Don and Jane said that I had to make my own choice but cautioned that they thought I was playing with fire. The way to deal with any kind of fear was to face it and to go into it, not to run, they said.

Looking back, I don't know if what I did was from needing to take a break, looking for some other way to do things, or whether I was running away from my fear. In the long run of life it hasn't mattered. The point is that I quit going for a while.

The first Sunday I missed was strange, and I felt totally weirded out. I almost got in the car and drove up but made myself stay put. I reasoned that I needed to not go if I found it so hard not to attend class.

The second Sunday I didn't find the drive to go, but I was depressed the whole weekend—severely depressed. Plus, Jenna and Leroy had gotten on me, saying that they thought I was having a breakdown, because I was too good at jujitsu not to be there. No matter how hard I tried to explain things to them, they just didn't get it. I felt a distance growing between Jenna and me, and that didn't help the depression.

I was to meet them for lunch after that second Sunday. I was standing around outside the restaurant, taking in the last of the summer weather and they were just pulling up when it happened. One moment I was taking in a sense of deep love and practicing sending it back out to everyone around; the next moment a young woman came storming out of the restaurant.

She was angry and crying, and just as she got a couple of steps away, a man came out behind her, yelling, "Don't walk away from me. No girl walks out on me." He was grabbing at her, and before I knew what I was doing I was headed toward them. I thought of my vow and was trying to stop myself when he hit her with his fist as he jerked her around and toward him. She went down onto the sidewalk.

"Bitch!"

His face showed a life of rage. I saw just the slightest turn in his shoulders and realized that he was getting ready to kick her. He was wearing work boots, and the damage could be severe. I still find it hard to believe how fast my mind worked in that split second.

I didn't know what to do about this. I had only thought of pacifism in terms of protecting myself. I hadn't ever considered the scenario of protecting others. I didn't have time to reconsider this option, so I acted. No matter what my decision was for myself, I couldn't just stand by and let her get hurt by someone who was clearly intent on causing serious harm.

I lunged just as he drew his right foot back, and moving just over the top of her, I plowed into him on his left side as he was standing just on that one foot. The side of my shoulder plunged into the pit of his chest just inside the shoulder joint and below his collarbone.

He went flying backwards and the kick never got off. He went down on one knee, and while I was saying, "Don't do it," he came up with his right fist cocked and, with his full weight behind the blow, launched it at my face.

I felt just as I had during my test. I was just there. No thoughts, no worries, just an emotionless calm, objectively reacting to the situation. I parried his blow with my left hand while I moved outside of him to his right side. My right hand moved into *shuto* (knife hand). In my body's mind, I knew that I could put him down without hurting, so I aimed the blow into the pectoral muscle instead of the clavicle and saved his collarbone.

My hips snapped left, timed a fraction after the blow, and he spun fast and went down hard onto his left side. He landed hard and rolled slightly back toward me, stunned but still conscious. I swung my left leg out and around in the axe kick position and stopped the kick within an inch of the side and bottom of his jaw. His eyes bulged with fear and he just lay there, frozen.

I pulled my foot back slowly and looked him straight in the eye. "Now you know how it feels. I could have completed that kick. If I had, you would have probably lost most movement in your jaw for good. Both joints would have snapped and they aren't fixed easily. Ask an oral surgeon, if you think I'm kidding.

"You owe me that jaw. And your collarbone too, for that matter. If I ever see you or ever hear of you doing anything like this again, I will find you and take back what is already mine. Now get up and get out before the cops come."

A friend of his, slightly hunched over and his head down in a submissive posture, helped him up. Then he and another buddy half dragged, half pushed him into a car, and they took off, burning rubber as they went.

I heard someone running up from behind me. I turned toward the street where the sound was coming from, my hands coming up in a defensive position. A detective was running toward me holding his badge in his hand. He held the badge directly toward my face, but surprisingly didn't even look at me. He went straight to the girl and knelt to see if she was okay.

"Ma'am, the guy who helped you ran off. I can leave you here alone and chase him if you want. He might get into trouble, though. Some people have been sued for helping other people." He never looked back at me, even though I was standing there, less than three feet away. She held onto his sleeve and said, "Don't leave me. Please don't leave me."

She wasn't aware that I was standing behind the officer. I knew that he knew where I was because of his studied ignoring of me. He wasn't responding like a cop who wanted to catch someone; he was telling me something, and I decided to take it to heart.

The crowd that was starting to gather hadn't seen anything, and they pushed past me to get a look at the girl and the detective. I looked over at Jenna and Leroy and nodded my head toward the street. They just turned and got into their car. I went over to mine and, driving slowly so as not to attract attention, I left the lot. I heard sirens coming from several blocks back. I followed Leroy's car across town to another hangout.

On my way over, I found myself going over events in my head. I had no regrets for protecting the woman and was proud of not hurting her attacker any more than I had. So much for pacifism: Two tries, two fight situations within a week. I needed time to think.

And what if I hadn't been good enough to not hurt him? What if I had done real damage? I needed to go back to the Dojo. I relaxed into the decision and joined Jenna and Leroy. As I neared the door, I put my arm around Jenna, and she looked up at me and said, "You've found yourself again. God, that was unreal. You are really something."

"He's something alright." Leroy added, "he's Attila the Pacifist."

"Shut up, Leroy." And then we all burst into laughter and made our noisy, but happy entrance into the diner.

eleven

Purple Belt

Multiple Attackers; Unarmed

I found the week hard because I was so excited to get back to the Dojo. I needed time to think, but I also sensed that I would need to be there in the midst of it all to better sort out what was happening. My first Sunday back was great; it felt like coming home.

It's not that I had resolved anything, and the image of myself in the Pit was still with me. But strangely, the incident at the diner had balanced my fear out a little bit. I felt a little calmer about myself. I hadn't lost control and hurt the man as I was afraid I would if the monstrous side of me got loose.

I had called Don and Jane and told them of the fight. They just joked and said, "You are going to have to be careful. For you, becoming a pacifist could lead you into even more fights." We talked some more and I had to agree with them that working out my fear of myself would be done more safely at the Dojo, where they could help me whenever the images and fears came back.

After just a couple of more weeks back at the Dojo, combined with some intensive practice in the back yard with Jenna and Leroy, I passed my Blue Belt test. It had gone as well as the Green Belt test until what was to be the next-to-last attack.

The attacker was to come at me with a knife. He was a Black Belt who knew knives well. He circled and then there was a blur. I barely got out of the way, but at least didn't get "cut." We used rubber knives with colored chalk on them so that we could see the strikes. Several more passes and I still couldn't get a strike on him, let alone a grab or throw.

Suddenly he stabbed high and then the knife plunged down. It wasn't much of a strike, but it ran across my leg and I knew that I had been cut. At the same time I got a grab on his knife hand and swung it back toward him in the natural action of the elbow joint. I was standing on the uninjured leg and knew that I needed to end this because of the "injury."

In real life, shock and pain are often delayed due to the changes in the body with the parasympathetic nervous system and the endocrine system. In real life I wouldn't necessarily know how badly I had been hurt, either. I just knew it had to end fast.

I twisted his arm quickly and lowered the path of the hand. The knife sliced across his throat, just as I had seen Don do so many months before on my first day at the Dojo. He collapsed on the mat, indicating that I had killed him. I saw the blue chalk mark on his neck, running from one side of his throat to the other. There was a surge of joy and elation.

I let out a loud yell that changed into laughter. Don and Jane chuckled, but some in the class, including Jenna, seemed startled, and I saw a look of concern or worry come across her face.

I stood there laughing, but was unable to stop. It was different than that first laugh, which was half yell. The first one was laughter at moving so well and feeling so good, laughter at the joy of being alive and getting to live one more day. But this other laughter was hollow and sounded nervous and inappropriate to me as I heard it echo off of the walls.

I was standing there feeling silly, unable to stop giggling; looking down at the person I had just "killed." I couldn't stop the release, and then I heard the rushing sound of the vortex and this time I was not taken inside myself. I was taken up near the ceiling, looking down at this maniac, standing with a knife in his hand, giggling over the death of an opponent. I got sick to my stomach. I was looking down on an imbecile.

An imbecile who loved to kill and who was training in a very deadly art. Then the roaring ceased and I was rushed back into my body. I was still sick to my stomach and ran to the bathroom and vomited. Over and over. I finally stopped, covered in a cold sweat, not just the sweat of a hard workout. I rinsed out my mouth and splashed water over my face again and again.

Finally I made it out. The class was mostly gone. It had been time to end anyway. Jenna and Leroy were sitting on a bench by the side talking softly with Don and Jane. They looked up when I came out. Jane softly said, "Congratulations on passing Blue Belt. We'll go over the details at another time, but most techniques were on the Black Belt level. Most importantly, though, congratulations on finding your shadow side again. You're doing well.

"Doesn't feel like it though, does it? Les, relax into this process and let these moments happen. That is how you will move through this."

"It's okay, I guess," I said. "I just don't understand. But I am going to stay here and keep going into whatever this is until I either figure it out or drive myself crazy."

"That would be a short trip," Leroy interjected. His attempt at humor fell flat, so he hung his head. "Sorry. I'll just shut up and sit over here." He feigned a look so pitiful that I couldn't help but smile.

We went home without much conversation. Throughout the week, Jenna and I talked, and then Leroy and I talked. Neither of them really understood what was happening to me. They couldn't see the problem I was facing. When I tried to explain the vortex, the Pit, and my image, they not only didn't get it, they looked worried. I certainly couldn't help them get a handle on it, because I didn't know what was happening, either.

I mostly trusted Don and Jane's reading that I was "going sane," not going crazy, but it didn't feel that way. Work that week sucked, too. I made several careless errors and my boss asked what was wrong, said I looked really worried. He was nice enough about it, but that didn't make me feel better about the fact that I was screwing up everywhere.

PURPLE BELT BEGINNINGS:

I began Purple Belt by listening to a short lecture on how to handle more than one opponent. Psychology, physics, anatomy, and some basic rules were covered in a thirty-minute talk. Then we began to practice. While there were new techniques for Purple Belt, the ones I would use in a fight were mostly the same old basic ones that worked for me.

The new techniques included some really hard, but really cool throws. I came to realize over the first few weeks that these throws taught nuances of balance that were useful in working against multiple assailants. The new striking and kicking techniques also were "icing on the cake" types.

The chokes and neck techniques were something else, though. The night Don demonstrated, all of us were stunned. I had seen them done before and they certainly had looked efficient. Experiencing them was something else again; it was chilling.

The chokes were a combination of choke and strike. Their effectiveness wasn't counted in seconds, but in fractions of a second. One stranglehold Don covered the first night was astounding. In less than a split second I was wobbling and ready to pass out. This move had apparently been used as a form of anesthesia for years in the Orient.

They didn't show us the neck-breaking techniques for several weeks. Feeling them, even though they were applied very slowly, carefully, and gently, was still really scary. One thing that was obvious was that they really wouldn't work easily on the street. They might be fine for the military in their work, but not in the civilian world.

We were told, and it was certainly clear to me, that this was not being taught for us to use, but rather to help us understand how the neck breaks and chokes worked so that we could avoid it during practice. My mind immediately went back to one of my first sessions at the Dojo when Jenna was teaching me and Jane had interrupted our session so she could stop somebody who was doing something dangerous.

I remembered now the position one of them had put the other in. They were moving to where the neck could break, and Jane had stopped it. Now it made sense. As Jane explained later, "If you don't know how the body can get hurt, you can't prevent yourself from hurting it. The more you understand, the less you will have to do when defending."

Still, it was really creepy. Even though the pressure was very little and the moves were very slow, my body knew instinctively that it was in trouble. There was almost an instant panic in my body, even though my brain told me I was safe.

We were not allowed to practice the chokes or other techniques without a Black Belt right there supervising. They were very strict; that was why their safety record was phenomenal for a martial arts school.

This was still upsetting for me. I was already so aware of how easy it was to kill someone. This, though, was way beyond other techniques. It's strange that humans are created so weak, and yet the things that would allow us not to hurt each other are so hard to find.

I remember trying to learn a pressure point on the forearm that makes the hand and arm go numb for a few minutes. I found it one time accidentally. I was practicing a defense against a gun and I couldn't get hold of the arm, so I hit it instead, and the gun just dropped out of the person's grasp. They were as surprised as I was. One of the Black Belts explained what had happened but told us that this pressure point was difficult to find and was in different places on different people.

Well, I worked on it and never could get it consistently. I wanted something simple that could help me not hurt people. It was frustrating. Sensitive parts of the body like the throat, eyes, groin, and kidneys were all easy to damage severely and permanently, while the parts that could help prevent damage were so hard to find. It was backwards.

I mentioned that to Leroy during class. Larry, the Black Belt who worked with us most often, was wandering by and looked puzzled. "Well, yeah. Why do you think it takes so long to learn how not to hurt?"

"It just seems morally wrong to be created this way," I replied. I wished I hadn't said that. It sounded really stupid. How could what we are be morally wrong? Another question to ponder: If God made us directly, then God was immoral. If this was from evolution, then morality didn't enter into the equation. This was going to take some thinking through.

I was having a good time learning to move against a gang. There was smoothness and a rhythm that was needed in order to find and capitalize on openings.

I was several weeks into Purple when the nightmares began. The first one came to me over and over in a single night, and I went to work the next day physically and emotionally exhausted.

In that dream I was walking into a restaurant and turned to someone seated in a chair. I just reached over and snapped the person's neck. I woke up in a cold sweat. I finally got back to sleep and the dream happened again. Three times in one night.

Later that week I dreamed that I was sneaking up on an enemy and broke the neck of a sentry. Then that morphed into my having broken the neck of someone who was just walking down the mall. No reason; I just went over and broke it, and the person died. Then I stood there and wondered what I had done and why I had done it. And what I could do now that I had killed in cold blood?

On and on the dreams went. I called, and Jane answered the phone. I explained what was happening, and she recommended that I come up that night after work. We set a time and I tried to get through the day.

I ate at a diner and it was then that the vortex hit—hard. Once again I was sucked down into that Pit. Once again I saw my face on the bottom and the hideous creature I had become. I was crying and screaming and hurt so badly inside. I couldn't get over how monstrous I looked at the bottom of that Pit.

I don't know how long this lasted, but I suddenly found myself coming to with someone shaking me. A cop was standing there, gently but very carefully shaking my shoulder. "Hey buddy. You okay?"

I wasn't sane enough to keep my mouth shut. I just blurted out that I had seen myself killing people and was trying to shake the memory of who I had become. He looked only a few years older that I was. He began talking to me and I realized that he was talking to me as if I was a fellow vet from Nam. "I understand, buddy. I have some of those dreams myself from time to time. Is there someone I can call? You don't look in too good a shape."

I didn't tell him I wasn't a vet; I just felt lucky not to get carted off to an institution somewhere. I gave him Jenna's number, and after a while she and a friend came and got me and my car. I just rode home in silence.

I cancelled with Jane, and we sat in my living room with me deep inside myself and pretty much unaware. I don't remember falling asleep, but I woke up on the bed in Jenna's arms. We were on top of the covers with just a quilt over us. It was the first night I had slept all the way through in a long time. I looked at the clock and sat up with a start.

"Its okay, Les. I called you in sick. I told them that you have the flu."

I couldn't even think or move. All I really wanted to do was to sleep. Jenna called my doctor and said I was feeling lousy and he prescribed some meds that she went out and got from the pharmacy.

I was in bed for well over a week. I had a fever, and every part of my body ached. It felt like the flu, but I knew that it was something else. The sickness was in my soul and had moved outward to take over my body.

I finally began to come out of the illness almost ten days after it started. I was still too weak to go to work and had used up almost all of my sick leave. As I had gotten better the last day or two, some of my time in bed had been spent thinking about what was happening to me. I knew that that day in the diner I had almost lost my mind, and I was very close to a psychotic break.

What concerned me most was what I might do if I did lose my mind. What would I become? Dr. Jekyll, Mr. Hyde … or both? I knew that Don and Jane kept saying that I was just looking at my shadow side with more clarity than most and that this was good, but I wasn't sure anymore.

After all, this had happened when I wasn't at the Dojo or just leaving it; this had happened out in public with no relation to what I had been doing at the Dojo. I was really scared, more than I had ever been in my life.

I wasn't sure what was happening, but I knew that I could only have one or two more episodes like this, at the most, before I lost it completely. Somehow the idea of sitting in a mental hospital was a fear bigger than I could imagine. I knew deep down in my soul that if that ever happened, then I would never come out. If I ever broke, I would never make it back. My soul would be lost.

I spent two more days off, which got me to the weekend. Over the weekend I found what seemed to be the answer. It wasn't that fighting was bad. As a matter of fact, Waboku Jujitsu seemed more advanced than any other ethical system I had seen, but somehow it was destroying me.

But that wasn't really it, either. The system wasn't destroying me, but rather I was being destroyed by trying to make myself into something I wasn't. I couldn't find myself here. The self I would find here would unleash the monster I had seen at the bottom of the Pit. I had to find a place that would be safe for me.

I had to become something else than a Warrior or a Warrior-Priest. I needed to be a Priest. A Priest who didn't fight. I didn't know what was right globally, but I couldn't go on like this. It wasn't a problem with the system; it was a problem with me.

I kept asking myself if I was copping out, but I knew that I just couldn't take any more. Even if I was called to be a Warrior or Warrior-Priest, it seemed that I didn't have what it took. My evil side was potentially too strong for my good side. I had to focus on the good side if I was to keep the monster at the bottom of the Pit and not unleash it on the world. There was only one way to do that, and that was to avoid fighting at all costs.

Pacifism came to the forefront of my mind again. But this time I didn't look at it with the idealistic view of my previous thoughts. I just knew who I was, and the more I let myself become involved in fighting, the greater the odds that I would let the monster I was overwhelm the kind and gentle person that I wanted to be.

Pacifism, for me at least, was not to be just a moral or theological philosophy, but a moral necessity. I would have to seriously focus in on loving people no matter what, or something terrible would happen. I would become what I had dreaded—since the third grade.

I was overwhelmed by sadness but also found a deepening acceptance of my situation over those two days. I made the commitment: I would die if need be, but better that than to become a monster. I even re-thought about fighting for someone else. While the woman at the diner would have been hurt, the police would have been there quickly and the jerk would have been arrested. She would have recovered.

Maybe my interfering wasn't as good as I thought it was at the moment. There were other options; I just didn't wait for them to happen. I rushed in, and in doing so took one more step toward becoming the wrong person.

One or two people getting hurt weren't anything compared to what could happen if I unleashed my monster-self. I spent the last few waking hours of my weekend thinking and re-thinking my decision, but I finally decided that it was the only path. I had the ironically amusing thought that maybe this *was* my Warrior's path.

I was called to die in order to keep myself from hurting others. I was my battle; I was both the hero and the villain. For the first time, pacifism seemed to be a place that could bring me peace rather than being an obligation of how to do life.

I felt both sadness and relief in the decision. But my focus was coming back, and tomorrow I would return to work for the first time in almost two weeks. Good thing; I had used up the last of my sick leave on Thursday, so Friday was without pay. Jenna was studying for a state licensing test for gym, dance, and exercise instructors, so I didn't tell her where I was in my head when she called to say good night. I just wished her luck.

She sensed something, though, and asked if I was okay. I told her yes, that I had made some important decisions and was finally at peace. She didn't reply for some time and then asked again, "Les, there's something strange in your voice and I have a really bad feeling. Are you sure you're okay? You're not going to do something stupid, are you?"

"Huh?"

"You aren't too far gone in your mind, are you?"

"You mean kill myself? No. I'm not going to kill myself. I'm fine. I just need some sleep to face work tomorrow. I'm not totally back to par."

"Okay. I love you. Take care of yourself."

"You too. And good luck on the exam. Call me tomorrow night and we'll look at getting together whenever it works with your schedule. I may not even have the strength to do anything other than fall asleep as soon as I get home."

"Will do. 'Night."

And with that I went to bed. Tomorrow would signal the start of a new phase of my life. For better or worse, my path was irrevocably set and I was hoping to make the best of it and of myself.

twelve

Pacifism Interrupted

Irrevocable Change

For having been sick for so long, I got back into the swing of work pretty quickly. My boss was glad to see me back, as were my coworkers. I know that it was genuine concern, but they also had needed to shoulder my load for two weeks. Most of the comments went something like, "Welcome back. God, you look awful," or "You've lost weight and you didn't need to," or, my personal favorite, "Whatever you had, keep it. From the looks of you I really don't want that."

I found myself thinking, "You're right. You don't want what I had—or am."

I quickly got caught up on where we were on the work orders and threw myself back into checking the specs on the steel being used in a ram on my current project. I was scared of making mistakes the way I had been just before I left, so I moved slowly and deliberately. While not quite up to speed, I did an adequate job. My boss dropped by after checking some of the work.

"You're doing fine. I was worried about you that week before you got sick. You seemed really out to lunch. I didn't know if it was drugs, love, or if you were cracking up. Now I know it was the flu that you were coming down with. Hope no one else gets it. A couple of the old guys like me might not survive it if a young buck like you went down this hard. Glad you're back—physically and mentally."

That felt good. I was on track, and while I had a lot to work through personally, I was going to be okay. The decision to commit to pacifism had been a good one. Still, it was a sad sort of peace that settled in. I guessed that that would be my life from now on. Still better than becoming the other version of myself, I thought.

Lunchtime came and I decided to get some fresh air, so instead of going to the luncheonette on the ground floor, I opted to walk the block and a half to a sandwich shop nearby. As I went out the door and turned right, the air bit into me a little. It had the typical crispness of a November day. Breathing in the cold, I felt my head clear and I could feel the strength creeping back into my body.

I crossed the side street, and a woman, walking in front of me and somewhat off to the right, slowed and stepped toward a van with its side door open. I headed off to my right to avoid bumping into her when I got closer. She glanced at her watch and spoke to whomever was in the van.

She started to continue on, but then paused, glanced at it again and stepped closer to the van. By this time I was close enough that I could hear her when she told them the time.

I heard the vortex coming. It hit me hard and fast. But this time it immediately spit me right back out to where I was. As I was coming back into this reality, I saw a man lunging out of the van and grabbing the woman. It all appeared in slow motion. She screamed and tried to back away, but he had hold of her wrist.

He slapped her, and then, grabbing her with both hands, began pushing and pulling her toward the side door of the van. She was screaming and leaning back, her legs pushing hard to get away while her body was twisting and turning to break free.

The man just kept pulling her. Then she twisted and managed to break free for just a second. Running away from the van, she moved several steps further up the block. He ran her down and grabbed her again with a full body hold. Half shoving, half carrying, he backed his way back toward the van. I realized that the vortex was gone and that I was just standing there.

He was still several steps away from the van when I moved. My actions were automatic and there was no thought. I was back into the no-mind state and just reacted. I covered the distance in a few bounds. His back was to me, but I had seen the pistol in his belt when she had broken free and his coat had opened. I glanced at the van as I was going by and saw the driver sliding over the passenger's seat and starting to open the door. Another problem to handle: he had a rifle or shotgun.

My body/mind knew that going after either attacker would leave me open to the other's weapons. But the man who held the woman had his back to me and didn't know I was there. If I fought the driver, the man on the sidewalk could turn and attack or shoot me. I couldn't take the driver out fast enough with him still in the van. My only option was the man on the street with his back to me. I had to take him out hard and fast and then turn and deal with the driver as he came out the door.

I cannot explain it even now, but my brain seemed to play no part in this inner discussion. It felt as if it was my body that knew and responded.

I guess that the memories from the Dojo formed the basis for my actions, but I responded the only way that I knew would keep me alive long enough to protect her. Don had once said when we were beginning Blue Belt, "Once you decide on a course of action, do it. The decision and action must be done in the same instant. In the world of the street, 'decide' and 'act' are one verb, not two." I acted.

I rushed past the man in the van and came up fast behind the man holding the woman. I slipped my right hand over his head with my fingers spread into a tiger claw, slid my fingers into his eye sockets, and jerked his head back and down. I stopped my dash and instantly struck the back of his left knee with my right foot.

As he buckled backwards I saw that he had released the woman and his right hand was now trying to draw his gun. My left hand was hard in a *shuto* (knife hand), and I drove it hard into his throat; driving through his trachea and esophagus and onto the spinal cord in his neck. I felt the trachea give way, collapse, and then crush. The sound of it was like a muffled crack followed by a soft groan, as air was forced out of his mouth by the collapse of his breathing passage.

I didn't need to look at him anymore; I could feel what was happening with him. His hand turned loose of the gun. I didn't see it, I felt it. I felt it in my right hand that had contact with his head and with my right foot that was in his knee. His body went limp before he even began the fall. He was finished. Dying.

I couldn't have seen what was happening to him anyway, though, because my head had already turned to see what the other man was doing. He was stepping down onto the pavement with his right foot and the gun was sticking out of the door, pointing away from me.

Before he could get clear of the door and swing the gun my direction, I had placed my right foot on the ground and took one large jump backwards onto my left foot. My right foot came up cocked.

I paused a split second to time the blow, and then shot it out into a strong back kick. My foot hit the door about six inches from the outer edge and the door slammed into the man. The upper corner drove into his face as he was stepping down onto the sidewalk. His full body weight drove him full onto the corner of the door, and blood erupted from his face.

He staggered backwards against the van. I could see the shotgun through the spray of blood. It was still in his right hand; he was trying desperately not to drop it and was moving it my direction. He was hurt, but not out—still a threat.

Behind me I heard a wheezing and gasping for air. It was coming from the ground and I knew the first guy was out of the fight. I focused on the van driver. I turned and cleared the door, shooting a lunging front strong kick into the van driver's stomach with my left foot, and he doubled over like a released spring.

He hit the sidewalk with both knees and his left hand. His right hand was till trying to get the gun pointed toward me.

He still wasn't out of the fight and with that gun he was still a serious threat. My right hand came down on the back of his neck in a *shuto* position, striking down hard and away from the body just below the head. I felt it separate slightly and his body go limp in the same moment.

His body may have been limp, but it was driven into the concrete by the force of the blow. His body bounced slightly, but with no muscle tension. It was more of a wave or ripples. Now he was out of the fight.

I turned, bringing my hands into a ready posture, and glanced inside the van, then around the street and back into the van. It was empty. And there were no other assailants. These two were down and out. One was trying to suck in air, but the attempts were getting feebler with each try. Blood was spreading across the sidewalk from under the face of the man nearest me.

He had no muscle tension and his chest wasn't moving. I grabbed the shotgun out from under his hand and pumped the shells into the van and then threw the emptied weapon inside. I went to the first man and took his gun. I emptied the six shells out and walked back to the van and threw it and the shells inside too. It was then that I heard the screaming.

It was the woman. She had screamed from the moment she had been attacked, but only now did it really come into my consciousness. She was behind me screaming. I turned and looked at her. She was backed up against a wall in a semi-sitting position. Her legs, still trying to get her away from this scene, kept pumping, but they were too weak to do anything other then add to her squirming.

A woman ran up to her and tried to calm her. She knelt down and held her. Several men came up to her and kept saying that she was okay and that the attackers were dead.

Dead? I already knew that on some level, but now it was starting to sink in. I was dizzy, but it wasn't from the vortex this time. I was becoming overwhelmed. Off to one side a voice broke through my fog: "Oh shit! Oh shit, man! What did you do to 'em?" I turned and looked at the voice's owner.

He was a long-haired hippy with a large metal peace sign hanging around his neck on a dirty rawhide cord. He was distraught and mumbling. He was either in shock or high—or both. I remembered running by him on my way to the woman. Peace symbol? Oh shit. What had I done? I wasn't going to fight anymore! And now this. I'd let the demon out without even realizing it. And two people died because of it.

People were dead. Because of me. But I didn't want this; they did. They brought death here, not me. I had been focusing on love. I had committed to die rather than fight, and now, twenty-four hours later, I had killed. Twice.

I was staggering toward the granite side of a building, hoping that I would find stability in its massive strength. The next thing I knew, I was leaning on the building with my left arm and my head on my hand, puking onto the sidewalk.

The cold of the building helped my nausea and I used my other arm to unbutton my jacket. The cold air hit me in the chest and it felt so good. I raised my head up and took in the scene. In the midst of the hubbub there was a silence—an awful silence from within me and from both of the former attackers. I came back in touch with my emotions as the scene came back into focus.

There were sirens and voices and sobs, but all that came out of the two assailants was silence. Inside I heard the scream that I had heard the first time in the Pit. It rose from deep within me and I noticed people turning to stare at me, startled and scared. There were flashes of blue uniforms and guns.

"Police! What happened? Who are these men? Ma'am, are you okay? It's the police. You're going to be okay now. Tell me what happened ..."

I heard multiple voices asking multiple questions and getting answers from a multitude of other voices. Cops moved people away, trying to restore order from chaos. One officer who was looking inside the van called out, "I've got two guns."

Suddenly police were searching bodies. One man in the crowd said, "The guns were theirs. They had 'em and were trying to grab this lady. That guy saved her." A cop was standing back slightly in case I hurled again, but he had his hand gently on my shoulder, saying at the same time, "Are you okay? Have you been hurt? Shot?" That last question came out after the other announced the weapons in the van.

I vaguely remember an officer with stripes on his coat, telling the cop beside me to put me in his patrol car and hold me for questioning. I was handcuffed gently and then put in the backseat of the car. He shut the door and I almost vomited from the stench of stale cigarette smoke and the smell of all the unwashed bodies that had been here before me. I yelled through the window and asked him to roll it down and turn off the heat. He complied quickly, probably hoping that I wouldn't make his car smell any worse.

Apparently, someone had eventually made sense of this mess, and a little while later, the officer in charge came up and told the other officers to remove the handcuffs they had put on me earlier.

"I'm sorry about the cuffs. We came up to a scene where there were guns and two dead bodies. We had to secure the scene until we could make sense of who was who. Seems like you're a hero by everybody's account. That woman who was attacked can't stop talking about you saving her."

"If she's got money, I'll bet you're set for life."

I must've looked pathetic, because I kept staring straight up at his face without blinking. I didn't want to see what was going on behind. There was motion as the ambulance crew covered the bodies and took them away on stretchers and as officers worked to hold back the crowd and the news media. I didn't want to see any of it. All I wanted to do was disappear. The sergeant bent his head toward me as he gently put his hand on my shoulder. "Look, kid: We are going to have to take you to the precinct for questioning by the detectives. There are two people dead and this is standard procedure. We have to find out what has gone down.

"You should be fine. Everybody's story is pretty much the same. Even the hippy agrees, although he's high as a kite. Still, if you want some free advice, don't say nothing else until you get an attorney. I don't see any problems, but just in case, cover your ass."

"I've been sick," I told him. "Flu. I'm not thinking too well. I don't know a lawyer. I don't think I've got a dime for the phone."

"We'll take care of the phone call."

"Officer? I'm his boss."

What was Mr. Hatfield doing here?

"I was coming up the street behind him and saw the whole thing. I already gave a statement to one of your men. Can I speak to Les?" He nodded toward me, his arched eyebrows framed the question.

"Sure." The car door had been opened when they took the cuffs off and I was sitting halfway out. I looked up into the face of my boss. I must have looked pitiful. I know my eyes were brimming with tears. "Sir. I was just going to get lunch. I didn't want this. I …"

"That's enough talk until we get you a lawyer. Do you have one? No? I'll call mine. And it's on me. I'll cover it. No, I insist. Jesus, man! You were unbelievable. I'm proud of you. I'm proud you are with us. You've got guts, Les. Look, we'll talk later, but I was in Korea. I understand. You're in shock. I hate to tell you this, kid, but it'll get worse before it gets better. But you will get better. Good job, Les.

"Now look, I'm going to go get that lawyer for you. Don't say anything until he gets there." He turned to walk away. "Oh. His name is Bill Sorenson. Top flight. He'll come." With that, he hurried off.

Proud of me? It didn't make sense. Proud of someone who just killed two people? What kind of a world is this? I was feeling sick down to the depths of my soul.

I don't remember the ride or even getting into the station. I do remember walking down the hall to a small room and cops looking up, smiling and nodding as I went by. They seemed to be on my side, like I was someone special. They let me call Leroy. I couldn't face Jenna.

Sorenson, the attorney, came after a while, met with me a few minutes, and said I was going to come out okay, but to be careful in answering questions. Told me things like, "Stick to simple answers. No more. Stay with the truth. Tell them so if you can't remember; don't make it up. Check with me if you have questions. Ready?" I nodded and he called the detectives in.

They were strange in how they were treating me. They had the reports already from the street interviews. They asked my story, but only once. They seemed sympathetic. The only thing they seemed to really be interested in was how I took out two armed men. It seemed simple to me. I had surprised them and hadn't given them a chance.

They seemed excited when I explained what I had done and what I was feeling during the fight. One asked me where I learned this stuff, and when I told him, said that he had heard of the place, but now he thought he might look into it.

Then it was over. They told me not to leave the area without checking in, and that they would let me know when the grand jury hearing would be. As we were all walking down the hall toward the waiting room, another officer came up and reported that they had ID'd both assailants. The two had a long list of rapes, aggravated assault, and ADW, or something like that. I don't remember the details.

I do remember the lead detective whispering in my ear as we moved on down the hall, "Nice job. You did us all a great service. Saved that woman and saved the city the cost of a major trial."

Strange how they could all see this as so great. All I could see was that my life was over. The demon was out, and two people died. And it wasn't just that I had killed two people; that wasn't the real issue. The real problem was that I had killed them while feeling nothing. Nothing! No remorse, no regret ... nothing. I hadn't felt a thing.

Everything was over. Even Jenna. How could I marry her if this is what I was? I had done it and there was not even one shred of emotion. How could I really love anyone if I didn't care about killing?

Jenna! She was in my arms before I could go any further down this train of thought. We had gotten to the waiting room and she was there, along with Leroy. They both looked relieved when they saw me ... and worried at the same time.

"You okay man?" Leroy said. "God, you scared the shit out of me when you called. Damn, I'm glad you're okay. I just left work straight out, called Jenna, and told her. Then I picked her up and we came straight here."

Jenna was still holding me, sobbing, "Thank God. Thank God ..."

There were tears in her eyes, as there were in mine. But hers were tears of joy because I was still here and that she hadn't lost me. Mine were because I knew that she had. The life I had hoped for was over.

And that included her. I couldn't put her in that kind of a life. She didn't know what I did about me. She didn't understand who I was. It was over. But we walked out with both of them holding me. And I was sad because this wonderful love, this wonderful friendship, had come to an end. And only I understood that. Only I understood why.

thirteen

The Ceremony Revisited

Healing Begins

Ted, I've already told you of the ceremony, of my coming to it, and how it ended. But I didn't tell you of how I understand it now. Or what happened to me across those four long months between that awful incident on the street and Jenna's Black Belt ceremony. Obviously, we stayed together, although at the time it wasn't at all obvious to me that that would happen.

The first night after I got home from the police station I just sat and really felt very little most of the time. Once in awhile emotions would just overwhelm me. Sometimes it was sadness mixed with horror and a sense of unavoidable doom, and I would break into sobs. I couldn't believe it had happened. It was like a nightmare that I hadn't been able to get out of since the third grade. Then after a while a merciful numbness would settle in.

At other times I was overwhelmed by anger at those two bastards. How could someone attack an innocent person and then put me into a situation where I had to kill them? They had ruined my life! Then I would feel guilty for feeling my life had been ruined when they were both dead. And then numbness again.

I went to work the next day and just plodded along. I worked much slower than usual so as to not make too many mistakes. What was the most difficult was trying to deal with all of my coworkers as they constantly tried to get me to tell the story and were congratulating me on saving the girl.

The rest of the week went the same way: plodding along through work; my boss checking for errors and correcting a few; going home, sitting, and riding the emotional rollercoaster.

Monday of the following week, Mr. Sorenson called and told me the date of the grand jury hearing. He told me that he had talked to the DA's office and that the DA was planning to make the case for justifiable homicide. Told Sorenson that it was "open and shut." Of course, I kept wondering what would happen if the wrong people were on the jury.

I hadn't made it to the Dojo. I just couldn't get myself to go any- where other than work, but I was especially avoiding the Dojo. The Dojo just seemed too overwhelming. What if I got there and found myself back in the Pit? What would I see there? I didn't have the emotional reserves to risk that. If that happened I knew that I wouldn't find my way out again, even if I didn't die at the bottom.

Jenna and Leroy didn't go either, that first Sunday. They just hung out with me for the whole weekend. Work came and went. Life came and went in the same, up-and-down cycle. Two weeks crept by. Then came the day of the grand jury hearing. I went, even though the DA had told Sorenson that I didn't have to. I waited in the hall outside the closed room. Jenna was there with me and hugged me when the news came out that it was ruled justifiable homicide and that I would not face charges. The grand jury took a break and, while out in the hall, several members came up and thanked me for protecting the woman. I tried to be gra- cious, but there was no life left in me.

My boss was there also. He stayed close while the people were talk- ing to me. My attorney had kept the news media at bay and had read a statement that he had prepared and I had approved. I didn't trust myself, so I had asked Mr. Hatfield to review it too, which he had. After the rush calmed down he put his hand on my shoulder and told me I would be okay.

He told Jenna, "Stay with him and give him time. The taking of life should never be easy. People who can do it easily are the ones I worry about. I was in Korea in a Ranger battalion, and I still see the faces of some of the people I killed and some of my friends who got killed. It took a while to get over it. Stay with him. He'll get through it."

This was a shorter version of a two-hour talk he'd had with me the previous week. I was lucky to have him as a boss, although I was too numb or still too much in shock to tell him that until much later. I did tell him that I didn't know if I could stay in this town with all the memories.

He said he understood, but that the worst thing I could do would be to move before I worked things out. "I know it sounds like a long time, but give it a year. It'll take that long to get it somewhat out of your system."

The day after the hearing he came by my office around 11:30 and asked if he could take me to lunch.

"Is this where you fire me and let me down easy by feeding me first?"

"No, Les. You're not being fired. You're being fed. Now grab your coat and let's get lunch."

We went downstairs past the luncheonette and he just continued walking out the door. He turned right and when we got to the cross-street he just kept going. I froze. He turned, came back to me, and took my arm in a no-nonsense way. "Walk with me, son," he said. "You've got to do this sometime, and now is as good a time as any."

We started off, and before I knew it we were at the spot. He stopped. I looked down and there was still a stain from the blood on the sidewalk. The chalk lines must have been washed off by the several rains we had had. I got dizzy and felt as if I were going to vomit. I tried to leave, but he held onto my arm and wouldn't let me go.

"Look at it. It's okay. You'll be okay. I'm here with you. You need to soak in the reality. Reality is never as bad as the imagining of it."

I stood there and I guess I soaked in the reality. After a minute or two, I began to feel a little more in control. The reality seemed less about my feelings and more about actually seeing what had happened.

Then he relaxed his grip and led me up the street. I don't remember what I ordered for lunch, but I do remember him going on talking with me and joking with others and me as though there was nothing different, like everything was the same. I can't say if this started the healing, but I do know that it made me know that my life would go on, no matter how I felt. I now knew that I could at least get through life. Maybe not well, but I would get to the end.

I had seen Don and Jane several times and continued to across the next few months. I never went back up the mountain, though. I would see them once or twice a week, whenever they happened to be in town. They would drop by my apartment or Jenna's and we would talk. It wasn't until several years later that I learned that they had been coming into town specifically to see me, not just dropping by when they were in the neighborhood.

Slowly my life began to get back together, one day at a time. Another big jump came one day when Don and Jane stopped me cold in the middle of one of my diatribes on pacifism and fighting. We were in Jenna's apartment and I was going on about God being love and how someone who was loving should be able to transmit that to others in such a way that they could feel it and be compelled to change. I wasn't someone with enough love, I said. I had failed God and the world.

Jane interrupted me, saying, "God *is* love, Les. God also created this world we live in. Think about it. In order for anything to live, a lot of other things have to die. Animal or plant kingdom, it's the same. Things live only because others things die. A vine slowly chokes the life out of a tree, starves it to death. This death is a slow one involving decades. Most predators start eating their prey while it's still alive. Some inject stomach juices into a live animal and digest them alive. How loving is that?

"But that's the world God created. It seems cruel. It is cruel. Yet, I still believe that God is love. Does it make sense? No, it doesn't. But I still believe it.

"It's called paradox, Les. Grow up. Get used to it. Nothing in life makes complete sense. Life is paradox. All of it. Quit trying to have the perfect answer or perfect life in order for you to feel good about yourself. We just have to do our best and trust God to clean up any messes that we leave behind."

Don chimed in, "It's called the problem of evil. Book upon book has been written about it. The Book of Job in the Bible is about it. There are no simple answers; hell, there aren't even complex answers. There are some approaches, but not answers. That's because we're finite beings dealing with infinite topics. Get used to it or go nuts.

"All that I know, Les, is that I would rather stand before God at the end of my life and say 'I tried' than to say 'I wasn't sure, so I froze. I gave up.'"

That was about all we got into in terms of ethics and philosophy. They spent most of their time getting me to grieve; they were my guides through the Valley of the Shadow of Death.

About three months after the incident, I realized part way through one morning that my chest didn't feel crushed and I hadn't thought about that few moments in time since I had awakened. I had gotten up and gone to work without thinking about it. I had gotten through the morning without thinking about it. And I felt better. Much better.

So then I felt guilty. Apparently, I told myself, I still didn't care. I was getting over killing two other human beings in such a short time, so something was very wrong with me ...

I was a mess! I couldn't give myself a break; I wanted to heal and then beat myself up when I started to.

Jenna had wanted me to come to her Black Belt test the first Sunday in February, but I just couldn't. I told her I would watch the video someday when I could. She was hurt and I was confused. On another level, though, that seemed to make no sense, because there was no future for us. I had tried to explain that to her but just couldn't get the words out. Still, in the end, I didn't go. I couldn't. I was too sick.

I hurt so badly that I had missed it, but I just couldn't have gotten there. I couldn't go back to the Dojo, where I had learned to kill. Back to where I learned who I really was. So I missed it. Leroy said that she was phenomenal. And I missed it. I didn't see her for a couple of days.

She called and said she would be over after classes and wanted to talk to me. She got there about 10:00 and told me she wanted me there at her ceremony. It was more of an ultimatum than a request. She basically said that it was time for me to get over it and move on.

It was her ceremony, her family was here, and I was to meet them. I remember her black eyes flashing; she had ended the argument by hurling the statement across the room, "That is the end of the discussion or the end of us!"

I couldn't handle all that emotion from her: her anger, her hurt, and the fact that I was deeply hurting someone else I cared about. I just couldn't go on pretending, so I just blurted out that I could never make a life with her.

She turned pale, sat down on the floor right where she had been standing, and broke into sobs. She just sat there, crying while I watched her, feeling dead on the inside. She was sobbing, pleading with me through her tears.

"Why? I thought we were in love. I thought it was going so well. What did I do? I've stood by all your craziness about this. I stood by you through the 'incident,' as you keep calling it. I've been there. Is it me? Am I just not good enough? Is there someone else? I don't' get it. I don't understand."

I felt a terrible pain in my heart and was really disappointed and ashamed. I killed two people, I had hurt myself, and now I was hurting the woman I loved.

"Listen, Jenna. It's me, not you. This whole thing has made me think all the way back to my childhood. Even that far back I knew that I was different; that I had an awareness of being damaged or evil or something. This has brought back some really scary memories. I haven't suppressed them. I've just ignored them.

"I'd been in several playground fights when I was in elementary school and junior high. Nothing major, but I had not only always been just scared of fighting, I had been scared of myself in a fight since the third grade. A fifth grader had started hitting me. I punched back, but didn't seem to be doing too much damage.

"He just started hitting harder and then suddenly I just saw what I had to do. I just hit him on the top of the forehead with the heel of my right hand and punched him in the throat with the middle knuckles of my left hand. And that was all it took …

"The rest of the year when his friends would see me in the hall, or on the playground, they'd whisper, 'Psycho.' I knew that they were right. I hated him at that moment of the fight and wanted to hurt him badly. I guess at some level that's normal, but I wanted to destroy him. And then, in the middle of the fight I went cold.

"And where had I come up with this way of taking him out? I was in the third grade and there were no martial arts movies in those days.

"So where did that come from? I'll tell you where it came from, Jenna. It came from within me. There is something in me that has always been able to destroy.

"Don't you understand? That's what's eating at me. I think I could have stood to kill those two guys if I had hated having to do it while it was happening, but first there was the bully and then those two on the street. Both times I was cold. Nothing. A big, fat zero in the emotions department.

"Jenna. It's not you. I wanted to ask you to marry me before, but how could I marry you when there is this really deep, really scary shit inside me? How could I relate? How could I love deeply? How could I love safely? How could you be safe? How could our children be safe?"

She was still sitting, but was breathing slower and her tears were slowing.

"So it really isn't me? I haven't done something to hurt you? Or us?"

"No. It's just me. It's about who I am." I barely got the words out. I just felt so weak.

"You think that there is something wrong with you?"

I nodded.

"And if you could learn to trust yourself again, then *we're* still okay?"

I nodded again, and she sat there studying me from under the tears. She seemed to center down and made up her mind.

"All right. Okay, then." She wiped her eyes on her sleeve, sniffed in a few times, sat up straighter, and then took a deep breath and slowly let it out. "Then I'm staying with this. And you."

She sat for a few moments. And even though I had convinced myself that I needed to go away for her sake and mine, that statement filled me with the first joy I had felt since that day three months ago.

"Les, I'm thinking that we just need to find the opening. You haven't gone to *no-mind* on this; you've gone to *all-mind*. We've got to find whatever it is that has you blocked from moving on, and then find the opening to get around or through it.

"I'm puzzled, Les. What does the bully have to do with this? You were a kid. You were scared. I don't know how you knew what to do, but who cares? It was a schoolyard fight and you both walked off, right?" I don't know what she saw in me at that moment, but her eyes widened and she drew back, stood up, and took a step back.

"Les, you both walked away right?

I couldn't answer.

"Les! You both walked away, right? God, please tell me you both walked away?

"Oh, dear God. You didn't! Tell me you didn't."

I just stood there staring. My throat was so tight I could barely breathe. I managed to whisper, "He lived."

She took another step back. She was fighting to control her voice. "Les, I've got to know. What happened?"

It felt like the vortex again, but this time I just listed to the right and fell onto the sofa. Jenna stayed where she was. My chest was tightening and I couldn't breathe. I felt like I was going to die.

"I'm calling rescue".

I didn't know she could even hear me, my voice was so clamped off, but I had to try.

"No! Please! Call Don and Jane. See if we can come up now."

"Are you nuts? It's ten o'clock at night!" Reaching for the phone. She said, "Okay. I'm calling."

And the muscles in my chest relaxed just a little. I don't remember the drive going into the house. I don't remember their faces. I don't remember what they said when we got there. But I do remember Jenna telling them what had happened that evening up to the point of the call. And then I remember Jane telling me that the time had come to bring the story out into the open; that I couldn't heal from having to kill those two men if I did not bring this story out and deal with it first.

"What happened in the third grade, Les?" Jane asked.

"There was this bully in the fifth grade who picked on the younger kids when we were on the playground. He would push us or shove us and sometimes hit us in the stomach or face. There was a place at the corner of the building where you were out of sight of the teachers. It wasn't a big spot, just a little place around the edge of the building. He would grab smaller kids and take them around there.

"One day when the teachers weren't looking, he pulled me around the corner and hit me in the stomach and I had trouble breathing. I was scared. I didn't know what was going to happen, but I knew it was terrible what he had done to others. I didn't want to have that happen to me. He said that if I didn't do what he wanted he would really hurt me.

"Then he punched me a couple of times in the face. I hit back, but it didn't stop him. I got more scared. Then I just went cold. And I wasn't afraid anymore; I just saw what to do. I just had to hit him on the forehead with the heel of my hand and then drive my knuckles into his throat."

I couldn't look at any of them and the silence just—hung there. Then Jane quietly asked, "What kind of things did he do to the other kids, Les?"

"He pulled down guys' pants—it was always guys—and pulled on their genitals and made them do things to him. The teachers never seemed to see it. Somehow they didn't notice that a couple of kids were missing from the playground."

"Did he do any of those things to you, Les?" she asked.

"No. I hit him before that happened." I was still staring at the floor.

"Exactly what happened when you hit him?" Don asked.

I knew they were all looking at me. I knew they were waiting. I just couldn't come up with the answer. I felt sick to my stomach. I thought I was going to heave. Jane reached out and put her hand on my leg, and said, "It's okay, Les. Take a deep breath and tell us what happened."

I had stuffed the memory down inside me for so long that it had come to seem like a dream. But I knew I had to tell them—all three of them. I knew I had to deal with it.

"I hit him in the forehead and then hit him hard in the throat with the knuckles of my left hand. I don't know if I felt it or heard it, but his throat cracked. And he dropped like a rock onto the ground, making a choking sound, and his friends ran off screaming. Then there were teachers, the principal, and then the rescue squad came and took him to the hospital. The police came and talked to me. Then my parents were there, and they talked to them, and I don't remember it all. I really don't remember it all, but I had to go see somebody once a week for awhile, and she finally said that she thought I was okay and no danger to anyone. But I've never been sure. So I just try to forget it." I still couldn't look at anyone.

"Les? Did you tell them what he did to the other children?" Jane asked.

"Yeah, but I don't know if they believed me."

Don picked up the questions. "Did the school suspend you? Were there charges from the police?"

"No, neither one. But some of the kids were afraid of me and the teachers looked at me in a strange way when they thought I wasn't looking."

Don said, "Okay, we'll have to unpack more details later, but I guess the question is 'What did your parents feel about this?'"

I sniffed a little bit, trying to clear my runny nose, and Jane handed me a Kleenex box. "Well, you have to understand my family. My mother didn't believe that fighting was ever necessary—that there was always some other way out. My father was supportive, but my mother was worried. They kept having these whispered conversations in their bedroom. She kept saying things like, "... don't want him to end up evil," and "How can we trust him around children in the neighborhood?" My mother's fears won out. So I wound up going to counseling. I went about four or five times, I guess. Then the psychologist talked to my parents and I didn't go anymore."

"So what did the psychologist tell *you*?" Don asked.

"She said I was okay. Told me that I was just defending myself. But it didn't make much difference to me, because I was still having the dreams of hitting him, and feeling his throat crack, and seeing him being rolled off on a stretcher, and then there were those whispered conversations about wondering if I was possessed or evil."

I won't go into more detail, Ted, but basically Don and Jane affirmed what I had done, told me that I should've gone through a lot of trauma therapy at that point, and that whether it was my parents or the psychologist who suggested the ending of the therapy, they were wrong. Jane told me I hadn't needed therapy because I was out of control or had anger issues, but because I was suffering from post-traumatic stress disorder—PTSD. They said that explained a lot of why I was having so much trouble with what happened on the street. I had to do similar damage to one attacker and it just reinforced the PTSD and expanded it.

I do remember them pointing out to me that if I had done that kind of damage to a child in school and wasn't suspended and the police didn't charge me, then they had to believe my story and that the level of my response was justified. They also pointed out that this young boy was a sexual abuser.

Around one-thirty or two in the morning, Jenna and I left to go back to my apartment. When we had first gotten to Don and Jane's, Jenna hadn't sat that close to me, but as I explained the situation, she slid over next to me and held my hand. When we got to the car, she stopped and gave me a big hug and said, "Oh Les, I'm so sorry. No wonder this has been so hard on you."

The next night Jenna, Don, Jane, and I talked for a while at my apartment. They listened again and Don once again explained some of my responses in terms of normal brain and endocrine system responses to fear.

Don and Jane made a couple of points they had made before, but they seemed to stick with me this time. I was overly sensitive to what I was feeling because of my childhood experience. I also was more analytical of my feelings than most people, and while this was good on some level, it was causing issues for me because of the PTSD.

I also realized that I was misinterpreting events. I was focusing on potential harm, not the actual good things I had done or the severity of the situations I had been in. Don said that he wasn't worried about the fact that I went cold, that actually that was a good thing. Demonic or evil people don't go cold or unemotional; rather, they actually enjoy it while they're doing it. I was starting to believe him, and by 10:30, when they left, I was beginning to feel there was some hope.

Jenna stayed on and the two of us continued the conversation until late into the night. The next day was Saturday, so it didn't matter how late we stayed up. We fixed breakfast around 4:00 and were still talking. We ate sitting on the floor of the kitchen. It now made sense in my mind, but I hadn't found a way to make sense of it on an emotional level yet.

Jenna looked up and cocked her head to one side. She was talking to me, but not looking at me. Her eyes were focused somewhere else. "Les, you've been afraid of yourself since the third grade. Because you were too young to understand and some of the adults who should've known better didn't help you, you have developed a strong sense of not wanting to hurt people, which is good. But, not getting the guidance you needed, you also came to believe that you have an evil side—or are evil."

"Yeah. Maybe so. Makes sense." And it really did make me feel a little better. "But then, what about my being totally cold when I do fight? That can't be healthy."

"Are you really cold and feeling nothing? Or is it more like you put your feelings on hold and then you do what you have to, based on the situation?" Turning to look me in the eyes, she continued thoughtfully.

"I mean, at the diner, you didn't do any real harm to the guy. An evil person wouldn't have stopped. And with the woman on the street, you couldn't stop there. To keep her alive and to survive yourself, you had to kill. Two men with guns took that choice away from you. Were you really cold and uncaring, or just emotionally on hold?"

"I dunno—maybe." I shrugged, searching for hope among the wreckage of my life.

"I mean, isn't that like what doctors and nurses do?" she said. "They cut all emotions so that they can do what they need to without having the strong emotions overwhelm them? Isn't that what you did here?

"You cut out fear and rage so you wouldn't over- or under-react. You went into a no-mind mode and did what had to be done. Les, you weren't cold, you were acting like a professional. You're probably safer and more in control in a fight to the death than most people would be in a simple verbal argument. It's just that you had to take the most extreme action because of the circumstances."

I began to feel excited. "But what about the demon in the Pit?"

The question made her pause. But then she got excited and said, "The demon that you see in the Pit is who you would be if you were full of rage, but you aren't. And because you know how evil that you could be, or anyone could be for that matter, you're safer than most people because they have never considered it..."

She paused her eyes flitting around a bit and then sitting up, excited, said, "I think your fear of what happened in the third grade is beginning to become a good thing. It's made this 'demon' into your Guardian, like, a guardian of your soul. It's a gift.

"It comes to you to tell you to become the best version of yourself, not the worst one. And your no-mind state is also *no-emotion*, and that is what keeps you and everyone around you safe in the midst of crises."

It was making sense. Maybe my fears were from focusing on the wrong thing.

"Could you ever screw up? Sure. But you know that, and that makes you less likely to. Les, you're better than most people, because you know that you can be as bad as anyone. Your vision of your demonic side is a gift. And you've used it well.

"You're not evil. You're not uncaring. And I'm not afraid of you. And I'm not worried about our children. And I love you."

She finished, drained and exhausted. She looked at me and I cried. Just curled up, rolled over on my side with my head in her lap, and cried. The relief valve had blown wide open, and all of the tension that I had carried for so long flowed away with the tears and sobs.

I was okay. I was okay! I felt it now. I was not evil. Instead, I was hurting because I cared too much, and if that was all my error was, then I was going to be all right.

I cried out the tension with my head in her lap. And when I was done I was calm. I still regretted having to kill; I still hurt over it. In fact, I still felt awful. But I had come to peace with myself. I was a good person facing his shadow, not a bad person trying to keep the lid on it.

Most importantly, I knew that we were going to be okay. I still had to move through more pain, but it was normal pain.

Soaking in the feel of her hand stroking my head, I found my courage. I sat up, asked her to marry me, and with her response of laughter and hugging me so hard that we rolled back over onto the floor, we became engaged.

Exhausted, overjoyed, and still struggling with the sadness and grief that could still overwhelm me; I had only a few days to get my courage up and return to the Dojo for the celebration.

fourteen

Purple Belt

Healing the Wounds

Wednesday. Jenna told me later that she had never been to the Dojo on a Wednesday before either, but had been invited to attend during the celebration. So I would return to the Dojo on a Wednesday this time. Jane had said to come with Jenna the next Wednesday and now that day was here.

I don't know if I was just ready to continue my studies at the Dojo, whether it was the different day of the week, whether it was Jenna's ceremony, or whether it was the talk with her father, but it felt like I might finally make it back to the Dojo. Maybe it was just that it was time.

Oh yeah, the talk with Jenna's father … I'd forgotten to tell you about that, Ted. It happened the same day as Jenna's Black Belt ceremony. Afterwards we had gone back to my apartment to celebrate her Black Belt and our engagement, and to give me a chance to get to know the family. They already knew Leroy well, and he was just one of the folks, so he came along also. Jenna's brother and sisters were excited about her Black Belt and kept talking about it in the car on the way home. Once there, Hank and his friend spent most of their time standing in the kitchen, hovering like two vultures over the snacks that her mother, Leroy, and I were pouring into bowls.

Jenna's father, Luis, or Mr. Moreno-Vargas, or whatever … (I didn't have a clue what to call her parents) was in the living room talking with his daughters. Leroy took the snacks of potato chips and dip out to the living room, followed closely by the two teenage stomachs, and the food was devoured almost before the bowls had settled onto the table. Her mother shooed me out of the kitchen as she started work on a lunch of cold cuts, a veggie tray, cookies, cupcakes, and sodas. I wandered into the living room, which forced me into talking with her father and sisters. Despite my nervousness, her father turned out to be easy to get to know. I asked what to call him and his wife, and he suggested Luis and Carol, if I was comfortable with that. I wasn't, really, but it seemed as good as anything.

He opened up the conversation to include me by asking about my work, and listened as I explained the projects I was working on. While our fields were different, as an electrical engineer he understood technical work, so we had a common ground.

Carol called out to the living room that she needed a few things from the store that she forgot to bring, and Luis (I never did get completely comfortable calling them by their first names) said that he would get them if I would drive, since he didn't know the area.

Rita said she would go too, but her mother told her she was needed in the kitchen. She wasn't happy about that, but her mother's tone of voice made it clear that she was to stay put.

I was beginning to smell a setup, and it scared the hell out of me. I barely knew him, and suddenly I was going to be alone in a car with him. If things got too uncomfortable, there wouldn't be anywhere to run, nowhere to hide.

I must have looked panicked, because he laughed as he put on his coat and told me not to worry; he would bring me back in one piece even if I was getting ready to steal his daughter from him.

He explained to Jenna, who was just coming out of her bedroom, "I can find out more about him and see if he is suitable for you and he can find out how kind and wonderful I am." Luis seemed to have the kind of humor that I've always found appealing. I studied him while he got his coat on and we headed out to the car. Jenna's mother was beautiful, and it was clear that Jenna got her dark brown hair from her mom.

But she got the rest of her looks from her father. She had his olive skin, along with those intense eyes that seemed to always return to a twinkle as soon as any other mood that had taken over had passed. I suspected that his eyes could blaze as intently as hers did when she was angry.

We got into my car and headed off on the five-mile trip to the only large grocery store open on Sunday in this area of town. We had barely pulled away from the curb when he turned and spoke. He was quiet and reassuring, but it was clear from his tone and his demeanor that he was going to have this conversation he was starting with me, even if we hadn't needed something from the store. I still wasn't sure if Carol really needed these things or if it was just an excuse to get me away. I broke out in a cold sweat.

"Les. I'm not going to eat you, so you can relax. Whoever Jenna picks is the one. You have our blessing and our support. Jenna told us about the incident four months ago. That hit her hard. She realized how close she came to losing you. She also told us how much you had struggled with it—that it had almost driven you over the edge.

"She also told us about the other night when you told her about not being able to marry her. It scared the hell out of her.

"It's okay, Les. It's okay." He gently laid his left hand on my arm while my knuckles turned white on the steering wheel.

"You weren't trying to hurt Jenna. You were trying to protect her— and yourself. She's tough; she handled it and got through it. Good practice for the future, for both of you. No matter how much you love each other, life won't always be smooth sailing. Every once and a while, it just rises up out of nowhere and slaps you in the face.

"I think that you two are a good match to go through the journey across the seas together. Storms are going to come, so you need to be sure of your sailing partner. Seems to me you're going to be a good team."

He paused and looked out the window. I was gripping the wheel and focusing on the road. "Les, it's okay. What you did. I know. I've been there.

"Right after school I went into the military and became a radio technician. When I got out, I became a police officer in Madrid. Just one week after they let me out to patrol on my own, I shot and killed a man while on duty."

He stared out the window a few minutes. He spoke with a controlled voice. "I was walking down a sidewalk, when I heard shots and ran down the block, took cover at the corner of the building, and then peered around. I was horrified. In a plaza, a man was standing with a pistol in his hand. There were bullet holes in the window of an elementary school that was in session.

"I radioed for backup while I ran into the square and took cover behind a car. I had drawn my revolver and I yelled for him to put the gun down. He turned slowly and just looked at me. I'll never forget his eyes. He wasn't there; he was crazed and he just wasn't there.

"He turned away from me, looked at the school, and very slowly drew a second pistol from his belt. He didn't fire, but started walking toward the school with both guns waist high, pointing ahead. I yelled for him to stop, but he kept walking. He was getting closer to it, maybe only fifteen meters away. I yelled again. He didn't even flinch."

That sick feeling in my stomach hit hard and fast. I sensed where this story was headed. I grabbed the steering wheel hard and focused, so I wouldn't wreck.

"He just kept walking, and then I saw him raise his arms slightly and extend one of the guns out to fire. I couldn't wait any longer. I fired. Twice. One of the shots hit him in the head and he went down in a heap.

"I was in neutral, emotionally. I just did what I was trained to do. I approached him and kicked the guns away from him, all the while covering him with my pistol. I was completely in shock. I did my job, but I was like a robot. During the whole time, I hadn't felt a thing after the first shock of seeing him standing there with that strange look.

"I secured the scene and the guns and kept people away for the few minutes—or seconds—it took for other *policía* to arrive. They took charge. The *sargento* came, took charge of my weapon and the scene.

"Officers spread out into the crowd and the buildings to take reports. I was transported to the station to get me out of the mess.

"I gave my statement there and was released from duty for the day. They sent me home to my family rather than having me be alone in my apartment. They had called my father. He left his law office and came and got me. He put his arm around me and walked with me out to the car.

"You know what was strange? All the way to the station, during the questioning, and all the way out while we were leaving, everyone treated me like a hero. But I felt horrified. I didn't get into police work to kill; I got into it so that I could help people. It took a long time to process what had happened and to get over it."

Shifting slightly in his seat so that he was turned toward me, he put his arm up on the back of the seat, and laid his hand on my shoulder.

"I'm proud of you, Les. You did what had to be done, even though it cost you dearly. I'm not proud of you in the way those who don't know how this feels are. I'm proud as one who knows what price you paid and are paying for your courage and your integrity.

"You are a good man. Never stop caring, or you will lose your humanity. Better to live with the pain than to not care and become something subhuman.

"I know you probably can't talk to me, since I'm Jenna's father, but if you need to talk with someone and there isn't anyone else, I'm here. I just don't want you going through this alone. When Don was talking about this in the ceremony, I knew he had been through something like it. I could see it and hear it. And Jane knows too. They can talk from experience."

We had reached the store, and the last few minutes of his talk we had been sitting in the parking lot, which was good because my eyes were flooded with tears. I finally managed to get out a quiet "Thanks."

"My boss, Mr. Hatfield, was in the Rangers in Korea," I went on, "and he has helped a lot. Don and Jane have helped a bunch. I'm glad you understand.

"My mother's side of my family doesn't, and I think I've become a problem to them. They don't call except to say they are praying for my soul. I'm not sure if it is for healing or for repentance and forgiveness for me, but it doesn't feel good. And my mother ... my mother isn't sure what to think. She's afraid I may be something evil. But—I'm moving along, so I guess I will be okay. I almost ran out of the ceremony today, but I stuck with it for Jenna."

On the trip home Luis was quiet. He didn't say any more about the incident. I understood that he had done what he needed to and it was up to me to come to the same understanding about what I had done. A question popped into my head, so I gathered up my courage and blurted out, "Is that why you left the police and came to the US?" He laughed and said no. He said that he had changed his mind about careers a year or so later and came to the US in order to study electrical engineering. He planned to get his degree and then go straight back home.

"So what happened?"

He smiled and looked out the windshield with that faraway look that people get when they are remembering back across the years. He smiled a very deep smile, tilted his head to the side, and gave a little shrug with his shoulders. "Well, there was this girl with long legs, brown hair, and a laugh that made me feel like that first dive into a lake on a hot August day. I met her just before graduation, so I decided to stay around for the summer just to see what would happen." There was a silence as he smiled, looking far back through the windshield.

"So ... What happened?"

He came back to the present and gave a little laugh. "Well, for one thing, a wedding happened. And then Jenna. Then another child. And another. And a fourth. And now you, Les.

"What happened? Like it does for all of us, life happened. And it has been very good. Minus a few days, or weeks, or even months that I could have done without, of course, but you can't draw all good cards."

And then we were pulling into the driveway back at my apartment. He had done what he set out to do. I got the bag of groceries from the trunk.

"Thanks," I told him as we headed toward the front door. "I didn't know what you all would think. I didn't want you thinking that I was some kind of monster. I ..." My voice choked off as the tears came. I stood there trying to hold onto the groceries and myself at the same time.

He put his arm around my shoulders, nodding his head slowly as he looked a long way away into another place and time. And then he did a strange, wonderful thing. He turned, took my face in both of his hands, leaned forward slowly, and gave me a gentle kiss on the forehead. It was a blessing from one generation to the next, and I felt it in the depths of my soul. He turned back and with his arm around my shoulder we walked into the apartment building without speaking.

One more step into wholeness.

I opened the door, went into the kitchen, and set the bag on the table. As Jenna's Mom thanked me, her eyes glanced over my shoulder into the living room. In the kitchen window I caught his reflection in time to see him smile back at her and give a slight nod. She relaxed slightly and I knew these in-laws were going to be okay. The rest of the day went great, but I couldn't wait to be alone to think over all that had happened.

I had made it through the ceremony, the celebration that afternoon where I got to know Jenna's family a little, and the talk with her father that day that I not only survived, but grew from. And a few days later, on that following Wednesday, I went back to the Dojo with Jenna. We had known that the Black Belts got together two weeknights a month at the Dojo. I assumed they were learning more advanced techniques. This seemed even more likely when we were told to wear our gis.

We arrived a few minutes early, and four others were already there. They weren't warming up; they were sitting on a bench near the wall, some of them talking quietly. We came in and we were welcomed warmly. I was the only one not wearing a Black Belt. It felt a little weird. I wanted to explain to them why I was there, but no one else seemed to need an explanation. They seemed to accept me there as an equal.

Don and Jane came in right at 7:00. They were wearing their gis, hakamas, and their red belts with the horizontal black stripes. They bowed at the door then moved into the middle of the room and began the ringing of the bowl. The others stood and we joined them in the ceremony of bowing and reciting the code of ethics. We continued to stand while Don and Jane walked to the other side of the room. They moved behind a table that had been moved out from the wall and lifted a large book off of it. We moved forward and sat on the mat in front of the table.

The silent, but measured breathing of meditation time began. I'm not sure why, but this time as I relaxed into this state, the image of the Pit didn't even enter my mind. It wasn't until several days later that I realized that the idea of the Pit hadn't even come to mind anywhere during the trip up on that night. How strange.

"Tonight we will begin with two quotes. First, a reading from the comic strip *Winnie the Pooh*: 'You don't believe everything you hear, do you, Pooh?' 'Sure. It's easier than having to think.'"

Don smiled and looked at Jenna and me. "Basic rule of the Dojo, and one of the few teachings that isn't really subject to debate: 'Don't let your ego trip you up in the search for wisdom. Take wisdom wherever you find it.' If what Winnie the Pooh has to teach is true, then it is as wise and valuable as teachings from Plato or Kierkegaard."

Then he shrugged his shoulders. "Plus, it's easier for me to understand Winnie's view of the world than Plato's metaphor of the cave.

"The second reading is found in *The Warrior's Codex*. It tells about one samurai's struggle with his anger and his honor …"

Two major issues were brought up: binary thinking and philosophical dissonance. They produced a great deal of questioning and discussion. Binary thinking reduces the options of even complex situations to just two. Philosophical dissonance is where one person has two sets of underlying beliefs that are in opposition with each other. They often go hand-in-hand.

Jane stated that we live in a complex world in an infinite universe. Yet, for the last 400 years, we have tried to reduce the answers to any question down to only two options. So when two people argue over religion or politics, for example, instead of seeing that there may be multiple ways of viewing the issues, people have gotten to where they can only see two answers.

Don picked up on that and pointed out that if we only have binary choices, then only one answer can be right and, therefore, the other must be wrong. If I want to be right, then I have to believe that you are wrong, so we are no longer able to disagree without becoming enemies. Differences have become reasons for fighting, not starting points for discussion. We have become intolerant of complexity and ambiguity, and yet that's the world we live in.

My head was swirling, because I knew that this discussion was being covered tonight because there was something that I needed to hear. Jane then went on to describe philosophical dissonance. Here, one person has two radically different sets of basic beliefs. The beliefs often come into conflict with each other and produce dissonance within the individual. This can reach the point of almost unbearable stress on the individual; the result often being either an irrational stance on an issue or intense anger, usually aimed at the person who brought up the struggle.

During the break Jane told me that one of the issues I was having was that I had put myself into a binary straitjacket in terms of war and peace. I wasn't looking for middle ground or accepting that the issue is too complex to have a just one answer for all situations.

Then, suddenly it was over. We stood and recited the code of ethics. As we walked out I was thinking that the class had only lasted about a half an hour, but when we got back to the car, the clock said 9:13. We'd been there over two hours. We talked on the way back, and I couldn't get the image of a binary straitjacket out of my mind. I knew she was onto something, but I wasn't yet understanding all of how it applied to me.

Sunday dawned clear and cold. The three of us drove up together again for the first time in months. I had the butterflies, but now it seemed to be a normal part of the healing process. It was time to return to practice.

We got there, changed, and class began. I was instantly back into the rhythm of class, but it was not the same. And yet it was. I now knew that I belonged here. But this time it wasn't some superficial feeling. It was more normal than that.

I knew that Waboku Jujitsu was a part of me and I just had to work out how I would respond to it. I had to find out how to use this place to make myself whole. I knew the secret to my peace would be found here. And in many ways it already had begun.

We got home and Jenna's parents called. She told them we had all gone up for practice.

"He did fine. He's doing fine." She smiled at me and mouthed "Dad." I let out a long breath that I didn't know I had been holding and felt a centering.

It wasn't many weeks before I was ready to test for my Purple Belt—at least, I was ready in terms of knowledge and skills, but I felt I needed more time for my emotions to settle around this next level of training. Don and Jane listened and accepted my feelings about it. "Why don't you do Brown and Purple together when you're ready?" Don suggested.

I hadn't thought of that option, but it seemed right. So after only a few weeks back at the Dojo, I began the study of our art with a focus on defending others and defending without causing harm. Ironic that I should study this now.

But it wouldn't have mattered. I had begun to believe what I now know to be true: there had been no other options that day on the street. What was—was. What I did, I did. Constantly second-guessing myself would be a short pathway to insanity.

Reviewing the options so that I could learn from them was something different than second-guessing. I had already done this several times with Don and Jane, once with Mr. Hatfield, once with Luis on a visit several weeks after the ceremony, and of course, a lot of times by myself.

If there had been other openings that could have led to something less deadly, I didn't see them, and I did my best at the time. Having listened to the descriptions of what happened from both me and my boss, Don and Jane were convinced that there were no other options.

I still wasn't certain, so one night, three or four weeks after returning to practice, I hung around afterwards until everyone was gone except our trio and Don and Jane. I asked them if there had been anything else I could do. They had me position Leroy, Jenna, and Don at the right distances and locations to re-enact what happened that day.

I moved them through what had happened. It was not hard to recall, as every moment of that time was indelibly etched in my memory. Then I looked Don straight in the face and asked, point-blank, "What would you have done?"

He looked at me, studying my face, made up his mind about something, and answered me. "I don't know. I wasn't there. But if you are asking if you missed an opening, I'd say none that I can see. I think that you moved as best you could.

"You did the least damage possible, but in this case there were two armed men separated from you and each other by a considerable distance, with a car and a victim, both of which they could use as shields.

"You were skilled, yes, but also just plain lucky to have found the openings you did. The man on the street was going for his gun after you grabbed him and before you struck his throat. He had no intentions of giving up. He intended to get to her by killing you. He lost.

"The man in the van? He was coming out to blow you away. He wouldn't quit, no matter how badly he was hurt. As long as he was living, he kept trying to kill you and get to her. He also lost. Their choice. Their loss.

"You had to stop them. Sometimes that means killing; sometimes it doesn't. This time it did. I don't see anything else you could have done."

"But would you have done the same things?"

He looked long and hard at me, shifted his gaze to the ground for a while. He slowly looked back up into my eyes and quietly said, "I don't know. I wasn't there. Technique-wise, I probably would have done something similar. But make no mistake: they would not have given in to me or anyone else. Whoever was there would have had to take them out all the way or die themselves.

"You chose well. You are alive. Your fiancée isn't grieving, nor are your friends and family. None of them would have deserved to do so. The woman is alive. Her friends and family are relieved and grateful, not sad and stunned. The two men died by their own choice. If they hadn't chosen to attack, to abduct, they wouldn't have died. Decisions have consequences. Carry the consequences of *your* bad decisions, not someone else's. You decided well. You lived well. Turn it loose."

So ... it had been good enough. I was, in that moment, all that I could have been, the best that I could be at that time. Now, years later, I know that there were no other openings that could have been found—not because there might not have been on some other day and time, but simply because there weren't. Not in that reality, on that day. So now it was time for me to move on.

Moving on: it sounds like something that starts at a specific point in time, but looking back, I don't know when or where it happened. I don't know really what caused it, but at some point I had turned the corner, and from that moment on my life was set in a totally different direction, and I would not look back.

I had not resolved for all time the issues of war and peace, fighting and pacifism. But I resolved them for *me*. Here, at this Dojo, I was finding out who I was. I didn't know how that fit into the big picture, but I knew that it fit into mine. I was threading my way through a story that, at the time, I didn't even know had been written for me.

Strange, isn't it? We are all part of a story written for us long before we were born. And without knowing the plot or who all the characters will be, we help pen our lives into the greater book of life and thus, in our stumblings and successes, write the story of ourselves.

If we do it really well, it will be good enough to be told at campfires across the ages. If not, then we have God to turn to for mercy.

fifteen

Brown Belt Beginnings

Defending Without Harm/ Defending Others

"You will have to learn to fight within a rapidly shifting, multi-focused center."

—*Don*

As an engineer I understood the math of what Don was saying ... well, at least theoretically. But it made no sense to me in how it would be carried out in the real world. I didn't even understand what he meant in the context of a fight.

And it got worse. By the end of the session I felt like a rank beginner. This was going to be a lot harder than I had thought.

The techniques were simple enough, but staying centered was hard. There were multiple centers: mine, the assailant's, and the victim's. I had to protect the victim(s) and myself. It was hard. I might still use a technique that I would when defending just myself, but now I had to consider where the assailant was going to go and where and when the victim might be landing, falling, or running. This turned out to be more complicated than any belt before, even though the new techniques were fewer and in some ways much easier.

The hardest part of Brown Belt wasn't learning to shield the victim from the attacker; it wasn't even learning to re-think centers. The hardest part was to expand my consciousness beyond myself, learning to include the awareness and emotional states of others while staying centered within myself.

That meant staying centered in who I was and what my role was. And most importantly, it meant giving up the fear of death while in the presence of death: being neutral in relating to death and letting it happen as it must; accepting its presence without worrying about its having appeared in a situation. I even had to learn to give up responsibility for whether or not the victim survived. I had to learn just to do my best and turn the rest over to God, or the Universe, or whatever.

Without having innate understanding, learning these principles became just a case of doing it over and over: taking one scenario and trying ... then evaluating ... then trying again ... then figuring out the principle ... then starting over with something new. It was long and tedious work.

And it would be a long time before the idea of finding the center and the centers suddenly clicked with me. Even then, it wasn't intellectual knowledge; it was learned on the body level, and even this many years later, I still find it hard to explain it in words. It is one of those things that you just know.

The closest that I can come is this: with one attacker, you, the attacker, and the two of you together have a center. But yours is where you focus and operate from. With multiple attackers it's the same—but there are just more centers.

But when defending someone else you have to focus and work from two centers against one or more centers, depending on the number of attackers. You can see an opening and get through it yourself, but it is much harder when you either have to have a large enough opening for two or find two openings, either simultaneously, or one after the other.

The "Defending Without Harm" section was a simple extension of what we had learned all along: a lot of time practicing catches on the holds and locks, parrying or blocking, increasing skills and options. All the throws, old and new, had to be learned to be done with minimum impact as opposed to going hard and knocking the fight out of the person.

The new throws were all hip throws. Interestingly enough, some of the advanced throws I was learning had been learned back in Green Belt by the women, and some of my basic ones were now being learned by them. Jane explained in one class why this was so and how the balance difference between men and women made such a difference.

One was the sweeping hip (*Harai Goshi*). While I could do it and make it work, it wasn't as natural as it was for the women. In fact, this was the one Jane had done on Don that first day I had stumbled on the Dojo. He had attacked her with a front choke, and she pivoted and did this throw. I decided to try that defense, but it was hard for me to do. I was just too off-balance.

The women, however, just swung into it naturally. Jenna actually danced into it all the while she was being pushed backwards; it looked like ballet when she did it—well, at least until the person she threw landed with a thump that shook the building. The landing was definitely not ballet. I know: I had taken it a lot of times, and it was hard. Couldn't even slap with your hands—just your feet.

The strikes and kicks were fun. The hardest, though, was the stepping kick. I had watched Leroy while he was learning this. At first he has just kept either tangling up his feet or falling onto his face. But once he got it, it was cool to watch, and he said it was awesome to feel. I had no idea how to fly with it, but an earthbound version was what I had used that day on the street. Some of the upper belts could start standing still and within a second be ten or twelve feet away, up in the air and kicking someone in the face. I began to work on this and found myself in a variety of positions, all of them leading to sprawling on the mat. It happened correctly once, though, and I was hooked. I learned that, although limited in height, doing this in this form was great for practice. Once again, though, on the street you stayed low. Too many cracks, obstructions, loose gravel, and the like to take a chance. But even earthbound you could cover a lot of distance in a short time. It also worked well for defending someone else.

With a gang attacking someone else, the advantage was to come out went by, and then to be back on them from the opposite side from where you just came. One moment the gang is attacked in a whirlwind from one side, and then just as they turn that way, you hit them from behind again. As Don put it, "If you can take out one, and maybe two, before they even know you are there, you have gained both numerical improvement in the odds department and a tremendous psychological advantage."

I remembered that when I was just starting Blue Belt, I was one of three people chosen to "attack" a victim for a teaching demonstration for Brown Belt. Don came in suddenly out of nowhere, knocked one attacker down, then grabbed one from behind and took him out with a deadly combination move as he was quickly moving between me and the victim.

He was headed my direction, eyes intense and absolutely cold. There was a slight smile formed at the corners of his mouth. It wasn't a kind smile, but one that sent chills down my back. He quietly said, "Two of three just died. Now it's your turn." There was only the slightest pause and he followed with, "Or you can spread eagle, face down, NOW!" His voice was quiet, but full of force and power. As he finished saying that, he was already on me and had my wrist in his hand. I didn't even have time to think. I just jerked my arm away and threw myself down spread-eagled without even realizing that I was doing it.

I wound up lying next to a Black Belt who had been the second one to "die" in this scenario. He lifted his head up slightly and winked at me. "Good decision." The place erupted in laughter. I felt a little embarrassed, but still … I had been really frightened. I wasn't sure until I stood up as to whether or not I had wet my pants. My response had been really primal.

After the laughter and good-natured harassment quieted down, Don went on to explain the physical part, but then added, "The real victory here was that I was able to use psychological terror to save at least one of the attackers." One fairly new student asked, "What would you have done if he had called your bluff?" Don's voice was absolutely quiet and completely eerie. "I wasn't bluffing. He did put himself on the mat, but if he hadn't, then I would have put his body there." There was silence.

Now it was my turn to learn this well. Week after week I worked my way in. I felt totally out of synch with my body sometimes, but I kept plugging. All the advanced people kept saying this was normal and everything would just snap into place at some point, and eventually it did, on the night of Leroy's Brown Belt test.

I had said that I was going to take Purple and Brown together, but the night Leroy was to take his Brown Belt test, I offered to be one of his throwing partners. Just on a whim I said, "Can I do Purple Belt tonight?"

It wasn't a problem; the tests were cumulative, starting at the bottom and then working their way up. Since we had to do all techniques to both sides and give and take them, then Leroy and I could just throw and receive throws from each other.

Don and Jane agreed, and the test started. Leroy was his usual, highly coordinated self. Suddenly everything I had learned was natural again, only more so. I had seen this happen with others, but according to Don and Jane, it was due to the techniques becoming more body knowledge than head knowledge. That transition happened that night. So Leroy got Brown and I got Purple.

The next Wednesday, I asked a question that had been bugging me. "After my incident on the street..."

"Yes?", Jane answered.

"My boss told me that he had killed lots of times in war. Then the two of you obviously have had experiences, then Jenna's father. I mean ..."

Jane and Don just waited quietly with their heads slightly cocked to one side.

"I mean ... This is weird. This happens to me, and suddenly several such people pop up? Come to think of it, there was that cop, too, at the diner the week before that incident. Did I just fall into a bunch of people who have had to kill? This seems too weird."

"It's not, you know. Think about it, Les." Jane smiled reassuringly as she spoke with me. "Are you going around telling everyone that you had to kill? No. Right? So why would they? The truth is that there are a lot of people who have had to kill: some in war, some as police, some as civilians. And some of them healed and have done well. Some are still healing, and some haven't found their way out yet. Sadly, some never will heal. A few may even end their own lives because they can't live with what they had to do. Some die slowly in a bottle, and some end it quickly. Still, there are a lot of people out there. You aren't alone."

I hadn't thought of it that way. I was doing better, but I still was struggling with my emotions from time to time. I had gotten to where I could breathe again and even go most of a day without feeling the pain. But I still wasn't over it.

It was the last Wednesday in June when Jane told me she had a homework assignment for me, a written report. I had heard that they sometimes had people write papers, but this caught me off-guard. Still, I was willing. They had had my number all the way along, so this seemed reasonable. What stunned me was the topic.

"Les, we've talked it over, and we want you to do a report on secondary crime scenes: what they are, what happens at them, and what the survival rate is. Talk to detectives, forensic pathologists, or whomever. And look at some pictures."

"I don't think that I can do that."

"I think that you have to. If you want to get over this."

"It's just ... Well, it's too soon."

"No it's not. Do it. You looked at the actual scene and healed, right? Look at this and get some idea of what real horror looks like."

I said okay while sucking in my breath. She was right, I knew ... but I didn't want to go there.

During this time of training, the techniques became less and less important. The Wednesday night meetings became my focus. There I began to really grow. I learned a way of thinking that was broader than anything I had encountered before. I learned how much I had limited myself.

sixteen

Brown Belt Growth /

Black Belt Beginnings

Armed Gang Attack

On Sundays, I was still working on Brown Belt. I was still having trouble putting the multi-focus part to work, but I kept at it. I was learning the concept, but it really wasn't until I was over halfway through the Black Belt syllabus that it clicked for me. The Sunday after the test, Don and Jane started Leroy and me on Black Belt. They said I might as well join in and learn some new stuff, while I was practicing for Brown Belt. It seemed better than just practicing the same old stuff over and over.

It was interesting though: the more I worked with the Armed Gang Attacks from Black Belt, the more the Defending Others and Defending without Harm congealed for me.

I had been worried that the Armed Gang Attacks would be hard emotionally, but in actuality they freed me up in ways I couldn't have imagined. I kept thinking that I would learn some magic techniques that would have allowed me to do something different so many months ago, but what I found out is that there is little that really can be done in some situations. I began to see that I had done well.

The problem with defending against multiple weapons isn't the centers: it's the movements and rhythms. Each weapon has its own way of being used and the rhythms are quite different. Sometimes there would be two attackers and other times three or four. And the weapons always varied. So there were different weapons with different patterns of use, different rhythms in different clusters and locations in the gang.

Early on during the introduction to the whole system, they told us that we would be tested on how well we used the principles, not whether or not we "survived." The basic thought was that if you did the defense badly, you would die. Guaranteed. On the other hand, if you did it well and you got lucky and/or they got careless, then you might survive—badly hurt, but survive. During the test there would be several different sets of weapons. The techniques were becoming increasingly less important as the processes became more so.

Purple was behind me and I was working on Brown and Black. But I surprised myself. Even when the multiple weapons were firearms, it didn't shake me up too badly. I did okay. My healing was moving along. That's not to say that I never had bad moments or periods, but overall I was moving ahead. And there was no emotional rollercoaster like the one I had been on since my first Sunday at the Dojo. Most importantly, I had not found myself back in the Pit, and I was grateful that that was behind me.

I had been asked to present my report at the end of class on the first Sunday in August. What I had found out really shook me up. One of the detectives who had questioned me the day of the attack had been very willing to talk with me and provided me with a number of photographs from several cases.

I had had no idea what a secondary crime scene was. It turns out that a secondary crime scene is not where the attack or abduction first occurs, but where the authorities usually find the body. The detective put it this way: "It is rare that we ever find anyone alive at the secondary crime scene. All we usually find are mutilated corpses." The photos were graphic and I realized how sick some people must be.

The detective ended up by saying, "You didn't know this did you, that you saved her from this?" He threw down a couple more pictures while he was talking. "A long slow death, most likely. Maybe days. Rape, torture of all sorts, mutilation, until finally she could slide mercifully into death."

I had not known. Somehow, all of my worries of being a monster now seemed absurd alongside this. There was some small part of me that worried about myself, but this stuff … There was no way I could go there. I couldn't image anyone going there.

The Sunday I went to do the report I had the butterflies, but was not really dreading it. I just didn't know if I could get through the report in front of everyone. Workout went on as usual, and then we broke fifteen minutes early. The class seated themselves on the mats and on the benches around the wall. I gave my report, including handing around copies of a couple of the pictures the detective had loaned me. The phrase "99 percent plus are found dead at the secondary crime scene, and 85 percent are long deaths with torture" seemed to hit all of us. Jane asked where the detective had gotten the statistics. I didn't know, but he seemed sure of them at the time. Even if he were slightly off …

Jane pointed out that that was why they kept saying to never let ourselves be tied and/or abducted. If that happens, you are dead, and the dying will take a long time. Better to die quickly defending yourself than to die slowly over days or weeks.

I was surprised at how easy giving the report had turned out to be. Now I understood why they had given me this assignment. I had needed to learn how my protecting the woman had saved her from a terrible fate. I hadn't been able to see it before. I had grown up naïve, and that had played against me.

It also made sense why the police had been so positive toward me. They weren't sadistic or cruel or uncaring; it was just that they knew what I didn't. Evil does exist, and sometimes stopping it requires the killing of the person carrying it out. I had heard that a lot at the Dojo. It was part of the Code of Ethics, but now I began to understand.

It wasn't just that I had killed while protecting this woman, but I had stopped a real evil. And in the process, two people died. That part was still really tough.

And what of peace? I realized riding home with Leroy and Jenna that day that peace is a great goal, but one that the world is far from achieving. Perhaps this was the best we can do while we wait for it to come: train to do as little harm as possible; care when we have to hurt others—care deeply. But still do what must be done to keep evil from harming the innocent, and understand that this is the price for growing up and living in an imperfect world. Work for peace, but accept that, until it comes, there may be no other way than to protect.

Strangely this realization fueled my passion for this defensive art. I found myself working harder and harder. And I got calmer and more grounded in the process. At the beginning of Black Belt studies, Jane had told us that one person with a weapon may or may not want to kill you. He or she might be using the weapon to hide fear or to bluff you into submission. A gang with weapons, however, is out to kill. There is no other reason for them to have the weapons and to attack.

I thought of the two I had had to face, and it suddenly made sense to me. I had seen it in their eyes and in their postures, in their lack of any feeling or compassion and their rage; it was evidenced in their constantly trying to kill until their last moment. I finally understood what I had walked into the middle of.

On the second Saturday in September, the Dojo was sponsoring an all-day self-protection course for women. As part of the preparation, those of us who were going to be helping and serving as "guest rapists" did an all-day Saturday training toward the end of August.

One of the exercises was for each of us to be tied up and helpless. We couldn't move our arms, which were tied to our sides, and our legs were hobbled at the ankles. Then one or two other students were assigned to harass us. They began to hit us with some body shots hard enough to hurt a little. It was amazing how frightening it was; I just about panicked. That's not just a phrase—I thought for a moment I really was going to lose it.

Then suddenly one of the Black Belts would show up and take out the person harassing us. In some cases they succeeded quickly with no further harm to the victim. Sometimes it was harder to do and the victim got "hurt" more; that happened with me. Still, I was just glad to have someone there to help.

It drove home the point very well: we were training to help others who couldn't help themselves. And for the first time I understood maybe just a fraction of what that woman must have felt on the street that day. I felt almost proud, but mostly I felt relief, because there was no way that I could be really proud of how it turned out. I just had to learn to accept that part.

What I didn't expect was how angry I got over being helpless. Part of the class that day covered how helplessness could turn into controlling others, which was a distortion of power. Or it could turn into depression, which was anger turned inward—or it could turn into rage.

I now understood what Jane and Don meant when they said there was only one way to power. Controlling another person might look like power at first glance, but eventually it led to becoming harmful and dangerous. Real power allows you to be genuine, caring, and safe—but very deadly. I was coming to understand the difference.

Don and Jane were two of the deadliest people I knew, but they were also two of the safest. The two men I had to kill that day were just plain dangerous; they were out of control. They might have been deadly, but not in the same sense as Don and Jane. They definitely were not in the same class with people that came out of this system of martial arts. It was true that even the most deadly could die on any given day. But if they died standing on the boundary, then it would have been a good day to die.

And then the thought hit me.

"Oh, shit. I might have to fight again. And kill again."

And I realized that the choice wasn't up to me. There was nothing I could do about it. It was up to … well, I didn't know what it was up to. God? Fate? Chance? It was more than I could handle, because I suddenly understood what they had meant in the ceremony:

"You always wear the belt, even when it hangs in your closet. It is always around your waist.

"And even when it is in your closet, it can be seen. Seen by victims who need you and by oppressors who want you to be somewhere else. It is the hope of their life for victims.

"It is your salvation. It could also be your shroud. And you took it on willingly before you even knew what you were choosing."

And yet, I wondered if on some level I hadn't known all along what I was choosing. On some level maybe I had been responding to what I already was. Maybe that is why some of the teachings had seemed more like reminding myself of what I had already known.

I was an engineer, not a theologian or philosopher, but I was becoming a practical philosopher, at least about my life, just by being here, just by responding to this place and its teachings. And just by some parts of life that I didn't want, but that were thrust upon me anyway.

At some point, while all these thoughts were going through my mind, I looked around and realized I was standing in the center of the mats with everyone just quietly standing there and looking at me. Jane smiled and asked, "Are you ready to come back to us, or do you need a little more time?" And this time I wasn't embarrassed, just amused at myself, and as I moved off the mat, I realized what it meant to be gentle with myself. I felt good about it. Maybe I was growing some.

We went on and reviewed a lot of basics. Went over simple ways to defend. Spent time walking around cars, around corners, in and out of doors, near walls, through and past make-believe alleys, and reviewed all of the ways of being in the world we had learned during the several-hour special training required for Orange Belt.

We learned the differences in male and female bodies and how to best use them in fights. We reviewed how women are trained to give up and give in, to maintain relationships at all costs, even of themselves.

We learned how to start the attack gently and then escalate the power of a grip or attack as the trainee learned better how to deal with it. Over and over Don and Jane preached the need for safety. Just as in class we were responsible for the partner we were to work with, in the workshop we would also be responsible for their emotional safety.

We were not told specifics, but Don and Jane did say that several of the women who were coming had been raped or were abused as children. We were told what to look for in terms of serious breakdowns, and that a friend of theirs who was a therapist would be there to handle any issues that arose. The ideal result in that situation would be to get them back into the class quickly and let them fight their way into sanity and health. If there were more than one person with such needs, Jane and Don would also respond.

They also warned us that some of the women, when threatened as we escalated the "attacks," would suddenly break through their previous training on being nice and polite and then they might get out of control. There was laughter among some of the upper belts who had been through this before.

One said, "I put a woman into a head lock. At first she wanted me to let go, but I just slowly started squeezing and she kept whining. Then all of a sudden, she screamed and started flailing. Just like we taught her, she shot one quick blow right up into my crotch, and just as I was trying to get away from that, she bit me.

"Right through a Judo gi—a double weave! And her teeth had hold of my flesh tightly enough that I couldn't get away." Some of those who had been there were in hysterics at the memory.

Someone asked how they got her off. Jane replied in a really exaggerated drawl, "Just like you do when one of your prize hound's got aholt of another of your prize hounds. You blow hard in their ear, and when they open their jaws to pop their ears, you quick-jerk the other dog out 'fore the jaws snap shut."

That did it. We were gone. The idea was funny, but not knowing whether or not it was true really made us go over the edge. Class was temporarily undone anyway, so we all took a break. When we came back we spent the last half-hour practicing techniques as we did when we first learned them so we could recall what the trainees needed to see, rather than what we might do from instinct.

It was just like my first experience of falling at the Dojo. I remembered clearly now and with a lot more insight: the throws they used in order to teach us to fall weren't anything like throws they would use on the street. They were just tools to help beginners learn to fall.

That was what we were going to do: use the techniques as tools to the women's personal power. Leroy, Jenna, and I, along with a few others, agreed to get there an hour early to help with parking, registration, and other needs.

REGISTRATION

We were expecting about twenty women and teenage girls. Leroy and two others went out to park cars. Jenna and I were to handle the registration table. Don and Jane were there to handle questions. I was to handle checking off the names, and then they would move on to Jenna, who would collect the money for the registration fee.

Soon people began to show up and things got started. Some were laughing and joking with the people they came with. Others were fidgeting from nervousness. A few were quiet, deep inside themselves. Don, Jane, and Helen, their therapist friend, were moving up and down the line, talking with people and making them feel more relaxed.

I answered a couple of questions from one woman, but realized that the woman waiting in line behind her was studying me. When it was her turn I asked for her name at the exact moment she asked for mine. I was a little caught off-guard, but answered her, and in the back of my mind I was desperately trying to figure out where I knew her from.

"Oh my God. It's you," she said.

"Ma'am?" I was getting flustered and still couldn't place her.

"It's you! It is you! You're the one who saved me. I was hoping I might run into you today so I could thank you."

Jane moved in and quickly got her through the process and asked me to come over to one side with the woman. Don slid into my chair. Jane put her hand on my shoulder and said quietly, "Sorry that you didn't have warning. We didn't know. We would have told you if we had." She turned to the woman and said, "We're glad you came. Seeing you is kind of a shock to Les. He had a rough time with the death of your two assailants."

The woman looked puzzled and Jane hastened to assure her. "It's not that he had issues with saving you. He was just hit really hard by having to kill two people. Even though it was two people like that, having to kill people is rough."

"Yes, but what about what they were doing to me?"

"It would have been horrible. That's why he did what he did. He did what he had to do. He saved you. He would do it again today if it were needed. Still, the taking of life should never be easy."

I think that she said, "Oh. Thanks." Or something like that. Maybe it wasn't that at all. But I don't remember much else from that day.

seventeen*seventeen*

Brown/Black Belts
Finding An Opening

When you find that your enemy is yourself, the only open-
ing to escape through is on the other side of your fear.
Find what is making you afraid and go straight into it.
—*from The Warrior's Codex*

Jenna told me that throughout the day I did okay but was somewhat "unpresent." I worked with two women who were about my age. One was someone I knew from work. The other was a college student Jenna knew. I just focused on being the person they could practice techniques on. Jane would demonstrate something and then we would help them learn it on each other and then try it on us once they got the hang of it.

A couple of times I did happen to notice the woman I had saved— her name was Shamica—and then it would seem to be a long time before I would remember what went on. Jenna said that Shamica had done very well. She kept asking Jenna questions about me and how I was doing. Jenna laughed when she was telling me and said that she had finally told her that we were engaged. "Only fair to warn her that I might be preju- diced about how great you are," I think was the phrase she used.

Jane had talked with Shamica over lunch, and after the day was over, she told me that the woman had understood my situation. She had thanked me again through Jane, and said that she and her husband would like to have me over for dinner sometime, if I ever got to where I was able to do that. If not, then that was okay too, she said. She was seeing a counselor to get over her trauma and was doing well. This class was one of the assignments.

I, on the other hand, didn't do too well that following week. Things kept coming back and I began to think about the Pit more and more, even though I never wound up back there. I decided that I wasn't as far along the path as I had thought. Jane and Don had asked me (and Jenna, too) to come up Wednesday, even though there wasn't a class that evening.

We met at their house and sat and talked about my response to seeing the woman. I was truly shaken up about having gone backward in my healing. I thought I had been doing really well on my journey, but suddenly it seemed that either I had been ignoring what had been going on inside of me, or I had been way overestimating where I was on the healing timeline.

"Les, it isn't linear," Don said. "Give that up. Nothing in life is linear. As long as you judge yourself on a timeline moving from Point A to Point B to Point C, you never will really grow."

"For one thing," Jane interjected, "life is a series of false starts, great big gains, falling down and scraping our knees, then getting up and moving on. When we grow, it isn't a smooth curve upward. Rather, sometimes it tends to be either a very slow gradual incline upward with a number of backward steps, and other times a sudden rush upward in an almost vertical rise."

She hadn't said anything for a while and, glancing from face to face, I realized I had dropped down into myself, internally wishing that this would be the time I could hear the magic words to make me whole.

"Sorry, I just found my thoughts running over what you said." I took a few deep centering breaths and then nodded.

"No problem. Just wanted to let you take the time to do what you needed to. Ready to go on? Okay … The problem with the second type is that we rush ahead, making great strides until we are in territory that is unfamiliar and situations that are beyond our abilities. That's when we fall flat on our faces. And if we are lucky all we do is skin our knees.

"But we are problem solvers, so we get up, brush the dirt off, and look around. We get our bearings, stumble around a while, heal some, and get comfortable with our surroundings. There comes a point where comfort turns to boredom, and we're off again.

"You think, like most young adults and teenagers, that mistakes hurt you and cause you to fail. Actually, they often are the points that trigger the most growth. You don't have to be the best or even be getting better every moment. Sometimes, just being is enough.

"You think that you've lost ground or weren't as far along as you thought you were because you saw the woman you saved and it jolted you. Of course it jolted you! You should have been jolted. If you hadn't been, then you would be in denial and that really stunts growth."

They let that sink in for a moment.

"Les," Don said. He and Jane have a funny kind of tag-team counseling that really works on you fast. "Les, don't think of growth as linear. That only makes you competitive with yourself and others.

"'Where am I on the line?' you think. 'Point 5? Oh, my God, I was Point 6 yesterday! I'm going backward! But who cares? I'm still ahead of George. He's only a Point 2 and he's been there for several years. At least I'm better than him!'" Don shook his head.

"Linear is a fine model of growth, spiritual or otherwise, for beginners, but if you stick with it for long, it becomes detrimental to you and those around you. Think of growth more as an upward spiral.

"Anguish, embarrassment, success, joy, elation, challenges, worries, overextensions, stretching, and on and on: they're all just sections of each level of the spiral. You get through whichever ones are on that level and you're ready to begin again. And you go through most, if not all of the stages another time. Only this time you are on the next level up.

"You go through this process enough times and you begin to be able to accept it with less anxiety, because you know there is a light at the end of the tunnel. You've come up several levels on the spiral from where you were when you came in the Dojo."

I glanced at Jenna. She was focusing more intently than I was for a change.

"If you hadn't come to the Dojo, this terrible situation with Shamica would still have happened, but you wouldn't have been skilled enough to have saved her, and you would have probably died. I know you, Les; you would have had to try to help her. So you had come up several levels just to get to that point.

"You fought through the Pit, which gave you enough insight to be able to move on after you had to kill. If you hadn't gotten that far you might not have survived afterward. Have you thought of that?

"You've grown and accepted what happened in some ways. Now you have to work through this again, but on a higher level. You'll note that while it has shaken you, you aren't a basket case or walking around like a zombie this time. You are much less fragile. You still care as much as before, but you're stronger now."

"Les?"

"Yes, Jane?"

"Let the air out. If you hold your breath much longer you'll pass out from lack of oxygen, keel over, and spill your wine. That's really good wine and I'd hate to waste it. But if you can't stop holding your breath, I'll grab the glass on the way down. If I save it, can I have it?"

I found myself laughing in little chuckles, and then realized how tense I was. It took several tries before I could breathe deeply and slowly, but then I began to relax.

"Potty break," Jane said. "Get up and clear your head—or anything else that needs clearing. Too much insight at one time isn't good for a perfectionist." Jane looked at Jenna, grinning. "They keep trying to assimilate all of it—every little detail—and then wind up missing the whole point."

Jenna giggled, Don smiled, and Jane's eyes were sparkling. I tried to smile as though it didn't bother me, but it must have been a pathetic attempt, because I didn't feel good about it at all and the others broke up laughing.

Patting my leg, Jenna said, "It's okay, Les. I love you anyway." Sometimes she really pisses me off. Particularly when she's on target and I'm playing the fool.

We came back together and, as much as I hate to admit it, I had relaxed from their teasing. It still stung somewhat, but I knew they were right.

Jane started off. "Tell me about the Pit, Les. You said you were think-ing about it a lot. Have you wound up back there?"

"No, I've just been thinking about it. I wonder what I did see down there. I mean, I know now what I saved Shamica from, and I've even begun to accept that there were no other choices for me that day. Still, I can't help but wonder what it was that I was seeing in the Pit. I'm certainly no monster like those guys I had to deal with, but what was the Pit about?"

There was silence for a while. Don and Jane looked at each other and seemed to reach some unspoken conclusion. Don let out a long breath. Then he seemed to make up his mind about something; rather, it was more that they had already decided, but he was thinking how to phrase it.

"Les, this may scare the shit out of you, but we have been thinking that the time has come to go back into the Pit and not only face this monster that you have seen, but to also see the other sides of it. Maybe it isn't just a monster. Or maybe it isn't a monster at all.

"I know that that seems foolish, but trust us: there are a lot of things that you need to think about. You only saw one face, right?"

I nodded.

"And it was a variation of yours?"

Another nod. I could feel my stomach knot up and the tension went all the way down to the depths of my soul.

Don continued to speak quietly, but with a deep intensity, "There may be other variations of your face that you didn't see because you got hung up on this one. Les, none of us is just one person or even two opposing ones." He screwed up his face and said, "Binary thinking. Remember? Instead of just one, there are a vast number of possible persons that we can chose to be. And each time we make a choice, each time we face another situation, we begin to set ourselves toward a journey.

"Jane and I don't believe that it would be healthy for you to think that the monster in the Pit is the only other reality of you that exists. Maybe you need to find out all of the other options of who you are."

"Les!" Jane's voice startled me back into focus with its sharpness. "Don't leave us. You don't need to go there now. We need to set another time after we have prepared you. You need to learn not only how to love yourself in spite of your flaws, but eventually *because* of them.

"None of us was meant to be perfect, Les. We are all born with flaws, and it is these flaws or imperfections that give us our growth points. Imperfections in wood give an interesting pattern, right? We all have to grow where planted. The soil where we are planted is something that we have no choice in. How we grow and bloom is what we can choose.

"And the world isn't perfect either. Your desire for being pacifistic is both understandable and admirable. We need pacifists in this world to remind us of what we should be aiming for. The problem is that in an imperfect world, it doesn't work for everyone to be a pacifist. William Ralph Inge said, 'It takes in reality only one to make a quarrel. It is useless for the sheep to pass resolutions in favor of vegetarianism while the wolf remains of a different opinion.'

"Gandhi understood that, Les. He once stated that non-violent resistance would only have worked against countries with a conscience. He said that against Nazi Germany it wouldn't have worked.

"And as a matter of fact it didn't. Six million Jews went to their deaths with only a few acts of resistance from place to place. That's why Israeli troops today take the oath at Masada, 'Never Again.'

"And why do you think that the pacifistic sects have moved around the world? Every time persecution became too much, they move to a country where the freedom to live and believe as they want was bought with someone else's blood … What are you thinking, Les? You looked puzzled."

"Not really puzzled as much as just re-thinking things." I was aware of a tightness in my chest and let the air out slowly, relaxing into a deeper breathing pattern. "I had started to say, 'So pacifism is wrong and we must just accept fighting as the way to live in this world.' But …

"But that would be binary thinking again and the truth is somewhere in the middle. At least the practical truth is." They both were smiling and after waiting for me to go on, Don picked up when I shook my head, somewhat bewildered.

"It would still be okay to espouse pacifism, Les, but if you do, then be honest about using others to fight your battles for you. And if someone breaks into your house, be prepared to witness the rape, torture, and death of your family, or be prepared to call for help and understand fully what you are asking of the police who are coming to answer your call. In effect, from that point of view, you're asking them to go to hell in your place.

"There are a lot like you, Les: people who have stood up against those who would harm others for no reason. People who have had to hurt and to kill—thousands of them."

As Don spoke, it suddenly started to make sense. "So that's why it wasn't until after I had killed someone that I found out all of a sudden about the people all around me who have done the same. My boss … Jenna's father … Some other guys at work …

"Yes, Les. People all around you have done what needed to be done and gotten on with their lives. They don't talk about it with people they don't know well, for the same reason you don't. Just like you, they can't just walk up to some new employee or acquaintance and say, 'Hey, I've killed guys before.'

"Nor would someone say to his future son-in-law, 'I killed a guy once.' Jenna's father only did that because she had told him how hard a time you were having with your experience and how afraid you were that her family would think badly of you. He understood what it was like, so he told you his story so you could heal from it.

"That's what stories are, Les: they are ships to help us sail seas we have never been in before. Remember one of the readings last month from the *Warrior's Codex*? 'When you set out to sail the ocean, you can't insist on having a chart that shows every coming storm, every sunny day, and the height of every wave, so you can predict the course of your journey, because there are no such charts—only the stories of those who've sailed these uncharted seas before and can tell both of the dangers and riches. They can tell of the teachings of the sail and the oar, and of the signs of the sea. But they cannot tell of what you can expect on any given day. All they can say of the sea is that it is as it is and it will be as it will be.'

"And such is life, Les. That's what these people have been doing for you: sharing their stories so that you can heal and grow. They have bared their souls to you. Use these tales wisely, and do not waste them on self-pity. And at the end of your journey you can look back and tell your tale to those who are preparing to set out, so that they can learn from you."

There was silence, and then Don spoke quietly. "You are not finished with the Pit, Les. You saw some of it, but not all of it. You saw what you thought was a monster, but you didn't see the whole of what is there. There is good there also. Not seeing those sides has left you frightened, and if you do not resolve this now, it will eat at you like a cancer.

"Next Wednesday, you and Jenna come to the Dojo at 6:00 p.m. and we will guide you back into the Pit. You may fear it now, but you need go back there and find out what really is there... and you need to learn to love it. It won't be as bad as you think.

"We will start with a guided meditation on something else you need to focus on and then guide you into the Pit. We will go with you and be there to help you. Jenna can go too, if she wants and if you are comfortable with it. Talk it over this week and let us know if you want her there and if she wants to go.

"Wednesday at 6:00 p.m. You'll be okay. We'll be with you, and we won't let harm come to you."

We left a few minutes later and the ride home became the harbinger of the next week: a kaleidoscope of fear, relief, sheer panic, and any other feeling I could dredge up.

eighteen

Into The Pit:

The Multi-Sided Warrior

It was a rollercoaster ride of a week and I don't remember the details of it, just the wild ride of emotions. Suddenly it was 6:00 p.m. Wednesday, and we were in the Dojo, sitting in our gis on the mats, all four of us in silent prayer and meditation.

Jane opened a notebook bound in soft black leather, using a scarlet ribbon attached to the book's spine. For just a split second I could see the open page was handwritten. She began to read aloud.

"Les, you were led here. You trained here. You left this place one Sunday, not knowing what life-changing events were going to occur that week. You were faced with evil incarnate and chose to intervene on behalf of another human being. You shouldered a heavy burden that day.

"You struggled under the weight of the load. Your love for Jenna brought you back here when you thought you could no longer come. You came back home to the Dojo and took up where you left off. Still, you struggled over what had been thrust upon you. Healing was slow, but steady: sometimes moving forward, sometimes a step or so back. It was a normal healing.

"You did a report and found what the reality would have been for Shamica, the woman you saved, if you had not acted. That insight let you see what real evil is, not just the apparent evil you thought you saw in yourself in the Pit. Your healing jumped ahead as you saw for the first time what you had been preparing for here.

149

"Now it is time to see the other half of what reality would have been like if you had not acted. You have not yet considered what life would have been like for you if you had done nothing."

I was startled and felt reality swirling, although I knew I wasn't headed into the Pit yet. Rather, it was that feeling I had come to know ever since that first day here. I relaxed into it and realized how much impact the words she had spoken were having on me.

"Close your eyes." Jane's voice was soft, but there was no denying the power she had. "Think back to that day. You are in your office and you're getting hungry. You glance at the clock and see only a few minutes before lunch. You get on your coat and head down to the lobby. You decide to go to the luncheonette.

"You are turning right and crossing the street. There in front of you is the scene. The woman is called to the van. She glances at her watch. Suddenly it happens: a man grabs her. She screams and tries to get away. He strikes her and is carrying her back to the van. You see the panic in her eyes. And the burning hatred in his.

"You find yourself wanting to help, but suddenly you remember your vow: you will not fight. Still, she is fighting and no one is doing anything to help. They move away, because they see the gun. She pleads for help, but there is silence and stillness from all around—including you. You bow your head to pray, or is it so that you won't have to see all that life can be?

"You start to move, but your vow was made to God, and you force yourself to stand still. YOU WILL NOT FIGHT. YOU WILL NOT FIGHT. This isn't your fight. You didn't cause this. People die every day from violence. You cannot let this take you from your path of peace.

"You start as the van door slams. It pulls from the curb, squealing tires, and your heart wrenches. It's too late now, and besides, you promised God: you did, you know. You kept your promise. It isn't your fault. There were others. Others who were not called to peace."

She stopped talking and we sat in silence. The scene was so real. She spoke again. "It's two days later and the newspapers tell the story of the police finding her body. The pictures scream out at you, and what do they say to you, Les? What are you feeling? What would that have done to you?"

Sweat was rolling down my back and it stank. I smelled that bitter, metallic stench of nervous perspiration. I was nauseated and sick to my core, sick beyond nausea alone. This went deep into me, and I knew then, that if this is how it had ended, I would have never lived another day. I might have gone on with my life, but I would never have lived.

The rustle of Jenna's gi brought me to a thought I had not considered at all in the midst of all of this: I would not have become engaged to her. I would have withdrawn into myself and become simply a shell of a human: living out my days, wanting to die, but fearing to meet God and having to explain my terrible error and my terrible cowardice ...

Cowardice! I hadn't thought of it that way before. Not facing life on its terms would have been just as cowardly for me as if I ran away from the fight in fear, rather than because of a decision. Maybe not for everybody, but for me. For me ...

I couldn't clear my head enough to gather my thoughts. The sounds of sobbing were too loud and they interrupted my thinking. I found myself annoyed that someone was violating my process. So I took a deep breath to calm down and focus and barely caught my dinner as it came up my throat.

I retched slightly and managed to force the burning stuff back down into my stomach, hoping it could churn away there without trying to escape again. I didn't know if I could hold it back a second time.

As I was calming down I knew that the sobbing that had interfered with my process had come from within my being. I was sick: sick to the soul from the idea of letting someone else die like that. I was breathing fast and slightly in heaves, but I made myself calm down and take in long, deep, slow breaths of air.

The air was cold. I hadn't noticed that before. The Dojo was colder than normal. Thank goodness, because if it had been warm, I wouldn't have made it through this without losing it all.

"It's a dream, Les," Jane said. "That's all it is. It didn't happen. You did stop her from being hurt. You did fine. Shamica is okay. With every breath you take now, I want you to come back to the Dojo. Feel the cold air. Listen to the sounds of Jenna's breathing. Ground yourself in that. You didn't let Jenna down. You're okay now. Open your eyes. You're back with us now. Look around. Take in a long breath—hold it—let it out. Let your tongue melt into the bottom of your mouth and smile. Smile, Les. Look at each of us. You are okay. You didn't let her down."

I looked around and felt a tremendous weight come off my shoulders. I had not even considered this option. And now I knew that at this time, in this situation, I had acted as I should. Not necessarily the way everyone should, but I had been true to who I was.

I relaxed and smiled in a way I hadn't since I had killed. Looking back now, I think I may actually have relaxed more than I ever had in my life.

We sat quietly, and then the thought hit me: "Was I hypnotized?"

Everyone snickered, and Don said, "Les, you're such an engineer! Always analytical, even when you have just seen a truth you've never seen before. Everyone, slide together until our knees are touching in a square."

We all scooted forward on our butts a few inches and once we were touching and had settled in, Don continued.

"Close your eyes. We're going to go into the Pit—all four of us."

He was holding a Tibetan singing bowl in his right hand, the one they used to signal changes in class, and Jane was holding a leather covered striker in her right. I recognized the quiet ring that comes from rubbing the edge of the bowl with the striker. It got louder and louder and then the overtones began. We were all breathing together.

The whirring sound began and suddenly carried me into the Pit, only I was flying, not falling. My arms were out, my fingers touching Jenna's and Don's and theirs touching Jane's. We were all flying. Circling slowly downward toward the bottom of the Pit, where a light shone and I could just make out the face of the monster I had seen my other times here.

I wasn't afraid in the same way as before. There was something that had happened a few minutes before in that other experience that had changed me more than I knew. It was then that I noticed that monstrous face. It was hideous. I heard Jenna gasp. Don whistled quietly. "Damn. That's an ugly sucker, isn't it?"

The face glared at him, but it had no affect on either him or Jane. I could feel Jenna's fear and certainly felt its impact on me.

"Les, don't focus on it," Jane said. "Look at it with your peripheral vision and see it as it is. See all of it. You are focusing only on one part."

I looked to one side and saw that it was a whole being, not just a face. I had been looking down and had only seen the face looking up. It had a body and was dressed in the armor of an old oriental warrior. The face was hideous.

"Look directly at it Les. You too, Jenna. Breathe deeply and don't give into your fear. Open your heart to it. Ask it what it wants of you."

The question had barely formed in my head when the being answered.

"Only one thing," it said. "I am your guardian. I want nothing of you except that you notice me when I come to you in your dreams. I am your protector. I am here to help you know when you are becoming what you fear I am. When I come to you, heed me. That is all I ask."

My eyes had a hard time focusing, then I realized that it was turning away from me. And there was a new face. And then another and another. The figure continued to turn and being after being went by, faster and faster, until I could no longer distinguish them from each other.

"Ask them to slow down and show themselves to you."

As my mind thought through Jane's direction, the whirling slowed down, and one by one they turned and I saw many, many different beings. After some time I began to see the same ones going by. With that I started to float up and we all began to circle again as a group, but upward and toward the top of the Pit. And then we were seated on the mat.

I looked over at Jenna and she sat there with her mouth open.

"I don't know what just happened, and I'm not sure that I want to," she said. "Was this what you had seen? I mean, it's just exactly like you had described, but I just thought you were dreaming or whatever, but ..." Her words had been tumbling out, but as she ran out of breath she just stopped.

I looked back at Don and Jane. "I had only seen one face before. The others?"

"They had been there all along," Don said. "You just grabbed onto the first one you saw. It came out of your fear of yourself. Or maybe it would be better to say it was created out of your fear of yourself.

"The others are also you. Which ones do you remember?"

"Uhh... A helpless victim, an angry man, a raging bully and tyrant, a fighting victim who never wins, a paralyzed victim, an anxious person, an angry fighter, a verbally abusive man, a dream king, a non-judgmental Warrior, a split Warrior: two beings in one, half armored and half in a robe."

I sat for a while and thought. "These are all me, aren't they? Just different beings I could have become—or could become—if I had chosen or choose differently. And the first one is my guardian, the one who comes to me to say that I need to be careful, that I'm going off onto one extreme or another. It shouldn't be feared; rather I should fear ignoring it, for then I would become harmful in some way."

Don and Jane just smiled and nodded. Jenna looked at me and relaxed deeply in a way I had not seen from her before. I guess on some level she might not have been too sure of me, either … until now.

Jane said, "The last Warrior: the one with two natures. That one came to mind last because it is who you are. It is your true calling. Les, you are a Warrior-Priest. That is where your battle has come from—your two natures. I know that you aren't comfortable with it yet, but you will become so.

"And you too, Jenna. You are also a Warrior-Priest. Your time for struggle is coming, but it will be different for you. Your struggle will come as a positive into the priestly realm, but be careful, for it will ultimately put you at risk of your soul. You will know these times when they happen."

We looked at each other and Jenna took hold of my arm and scooted next to me.

Don spoke to both of us as he moved closer to Jane. "Do you know the story of Peter's sheet? No? Well, it's from the New Testament. Peter had believed that only Jews could be followers of the Christ. He wanted to have nothing to do with the Gentiles who were considered unclean.

"He was hungry and went up on a roof to take a nap until dinner. He had a dream, a vision, that God came and spread out a sheet full of all kinds of animals and said for him to eat. But many of the animals were unclean to the Jews so Peter politely refused, quoting the dietary laws of the Jews. So God took the sheet up.

"This happened twice more, each time with Peter telling God that the food was unclean. God then spoke to him and said, 'Nothing I have made is unclean.' Peter got up and went downstairs and there at the door was a servant of a gentile asking Peter to come and preach to them about the Christ.

"Only then did Peter understand the dream. There are a lot of other ramifications to the story, but the point for you is this—both of you, hear us well: Nothing God creates is unclean—nothing. So if you were created to be a Warrior or a Warrior-Priest, it does not make you unclean, no matter who tells you it does. Do you understand? You were not made unclean. Learn that. Feel that. Take that into your soul and write it on your heart. You were made by God and you are not unclean. Accept whatever role you were born to play in the story of life, and live it well."

With that they got up, and after a few moments of silence they led us to the doors. We put on our coats and went out into the night.

nineteen

Black Belt Test

The time had come. I knew it and was going to approach Don and Jane about doing both my Brown and Black Belt tests. That same Sunday they brought up the topic first and with their typical directness told me that since Jenna and I were to get married in December, they thought I needed to do Black Belt and deal with any fallout from it long before the wedding.

We set Saturday of Thanksgiving weekend, since my family wanted to come and that was when they could make it easiest. My mother was coming out of pride and support, but I think that she was also hoping to somehow put to rest her fears of me and mistrust for what I had learned and done.

My family had rallied around me quickly, if not always helpfully, and offered a variety of supports. My father was proud and seemed to understand the struggle I was going through. The only problem for me from his side was that the youngest of my uncles had that "they needed killing" mentality and had told me he was proud that I had "done them both in."

My mother tried to be supportive but kept saying she wished I could have done something else. "Maybe if you had talked to them…" Standing behind her, Dad just rolled his eyes, his look indicating that he couldn't get why she could never see the world as it was.

Now my Black Belt test was coming. My father's family were all coming. They wanted to see me and were truly proud, even if I'm not sure of the ethics underlying the motivations of Uncle "they-deserved-to-die". He actually asked if he was going to see some of what I had learned that let me "do 'em in so quick." All I could reply was, "Well, sort of."

Dad did call one weekend to offer to tell his extremist younger brother to stay home, if it was going to bother me. I told him I would think about it. I mentioned it to Jenna and Leroy. Leroy's comment was right on target: "You won't change him and you'll still have to live with him. You'll keep running into people like him who don't get it. Might as well get on with learning to cope and ignore people like him."

Don's comment was also short and to the point. He shrugged his shoulders and said in an exaggerated drawl, "Never try to teach a pig to sing. It'll only waste your time and frustrate the pig." I called my father and told him everyone was welcome.

I had one last task before taking the test: I had to talk with Jenna and apologize that I hadn't been there for her. She sat quietly and heard me out. When I had finished she smiled and began quietly, "It's okay, Les. I knew then that you were upset and crushed. I didn't understand it like I do now, though. As time went on and I saw your family's responses, I got a much better understanding of how much you had been torn between the two sides.

"And then finding out about the fight you were forced into in the third grade and how the adults responded in a way that added to your pain and misunderstanding of yourself made it even clearer. But when I went into the Pit with you that night—Oh, God! Now I understand something of the depth of what you were facing. Your not coming to my test really isn't a problem anymore.

"You lived through the fight and came back to me from the street. You lived through your spiritual fight and came back to me from the Pit, also. I'm just glad to still have you. I will be there at your test. You owe me no apology for not being there at mine. You were under heavy emotional attack and found the only opening that there was for you at that time. You did what you had to to survive."

With that I was as ready as you can be for such a test. It is not just a test of skill, but an endurance test. You start at the beginning of Orange Belt and go through all of the techniques through Black Belt. The test that I saw was set up in a different order than I had set mine up, but the total number of techniques is the same. Every punch and kick is thrown multiple times, full force, and with control. Every hold, takedown, and throw is done full speed to both sides, and you give and take each one to both sides.

All of the defenses are done, also to both sides. Defense circle. Judo and karate sparring. Multiple street attacks; whatever the attacker uses.

Every weapon defense to each side: forehand, backhand, overhead, thrust, uppercut ... and then there are the freestyle attacks with each. Weapon after weapon, defense after defense. Then unarmed gang attacks: two, three, and four people. This is followed by defenses against selected attacks, where you try to defend without harming the person. Defending others would follow, and finally, armed gang attack with varying weapons and numbers of attackers.

Then you sit exhausted and wondering if you will ever breathe normally again while you wait for the scores to be tallied and the results reported. I knew how tough it could be. I had seen one test when I first started coming. While it was usually no more than two-and-a-half to three hours long, what sapped you was the pace, the constant movement, and the intensity.

It was a cold, rainy Saturday. I knew that once the test was over we would need to get off the mountain, because once the sun went down there was going to be a lot of ice on the road. My family came and situated themselves around the wall. Jenna's family also came.

Jenna had asked me if it was okay for her family to be there; her father had wanted to see me test, but mostly to support me through this time. I actually felt a lot better about him being there than some of my own family. Not that I wasn't glad that Mom and Dad were there; I was. I really wanted them to see me. I wanted them to be proud of me and maybe somehow understand what this was about.

I was a mess of emotions when I entered the doors, but I was okay ... basically. I let Leroy situate my family while I went over and began to warm up along with several others who were going to help me on the test. A number of the students came in and sat on the mats around the edges. Don and Jane came in and introduced themselves to the families and then came over to me and chatted for a few minutes.

They then went over to a card table that had been set up at the far end of the room. They got out their forms and then the ringing of the bowl sounded throughout the Dojo. I stood up at the center. They asked the others if they were ready and got an affirmative reply. They then asked me the same question. I nodded, and the test began.

I demonstrated some of the basic blocks, punches, kicks, and stamps. Then we moved into the defenses. They would call out defenses and I would be "attacked" and would respond accordingly. The attackers were all upper-level belts, so I could respond as I chose and not have to worry about whether they could take a fall or not.

The test started a little slowly, but the defenses picked up the pace and the intensity. Part way through this section they asked to see some use of throws in defending, but only when appropriate to the attack. That was easy enough.

Then Green Belt started. I did the striking techniques, followed by the holds and locks. I like the holds and I prefer the circular style over the linear, although some moves lend themselves more to linear. I did a front bent-arm lock against a straight grab to the collar and turned it into a two-directional throw rather than just a take down. My opponent went sailing through the air and landed some distance from me.

As he landed, I was turned toward the bench where my family was sitting. Turning loose of his arm, I looked up into the eyes of my family. My mother seemed surprised and amazed. My father was looking at me with a definite sense of respect. My "Kill 'em all, let God do the sorting" uncle was impressed in a "way to go, kid" kind of a way.

I had a sudden feeling of both revulsion and sadness to the point of pity for him. I realized for the first time that here was someone who was weak on the inside. I don't know if it was that he was actually afraid of life, or whether on some level he cared a lot about people but also wanted to be a hero, a "real man." As I turned back to the mat for the next technique, I knew the answer. He was a deeply caring man who had a very sensitive side that I had seen several times in my life.

When my grandmother died, he had disappeared during visiting hours from the funeral home for a while. He came back with red eyes and the smell of alcohol on his breath. I knew now what his situation was. He cared so deeply and yet wanted to be able to fight. It was the dissonance within that was keeping him from being real. He would always be a fighter rather than a Warrior if he didn't solve this. I could have been like him if I hadn't happened on the Dojo.

The next move was happening and I refocused on the task. It was several more moves before I had a moment to think on about this. I realized that I wished he could study here to relieve his pain, and it was then that I knew that there were pains that were more serious than personal struggle. Dissonance must be far worse, because it drives you more and more into extremism.

We were now into the throws. I could write up the order of my test as I wanted and I had set up all the hip throws at once. I did the basics and then moved to *Harai goshi* (the sweeping hip throw). This one is easier for women and was my weakest one. I planned it first among the advanced throws.

I got through it okay and then swung into some of my favorites, including *Tsuri goshi* (the collar hip throw). I don't know why I liked this throw so much, but there was something so fast about it, and it worked so well when being pushed backwards by someone bigger. I'm about 5'10" and 185, so there are a lot of people bigger than I am. The person who came after me was a former all-star defensive lineman, and he just charged straight into me, grabbing my gi collars as he came.

I was just getting ready to turn for the throw when my feet went off the mat. If I threw him he would land very hard on the wood floor, so I just floated backward and yelled out, "Break!" In the Dojo safety is always first and we are not just allowed to stop a technique where we could hurt someone, it is a requirement. I could have completed the throw, but they would have probably flunked me on the spot. Control is harder than going through with whatever you started. This "break" meant that I was fully aware of all of my surroundings and was reacting ahead of where I was.

They called us back to the far end of the mat and we started over. He rushed again and grabbed me. This time he actually lifted me up and ran so fast with me in the air that once again we were off the mat. I yelled out again.

Everyone was laughing. Don said, "Les, what would you have done?" We were still in position except that my feet were now back on the ground, but we weren't moving, so I immediately kicked into his groin, while striking into his eyes. Jane told me I was fine and we would try it again. Laughing, she told Bill, my attacker, "Les isn't a bag of potatoes or a quarterback. Just attack him and grab, don't run over him." Bill looked a little embarrassed, nodded okay, and we went way back off the other end.

This time it worked. As soon as my feet touched the mat—at least they were touching this time—I pivoted and drove my elbow into his shoulder while dropping my hips. As his momentum carried him forward, I stepped forward a little to maintain balance and then snapped my hips up. He went over fast and hard. He landed well, popped right back up, and instantly hit me again, only to the other side, and I nailed him again.

He got up and another student came onto the mat. I noticed Jane and Don's smiles and as I turned; I couldn't help myself. I looked over my family and saw both surprised looks and pride. I didn't stop looking until I was looking straight at Luis. He was looking at me and I know he was aware that I was searching him to see what he thought. He had an intense look, but one of pride and understanding. He gave me just the slightest smile and a nod.

Things were going well. I worked my way through the belts and techniques. Unarmed gang attack went well, but not perfectly. Weapons went well. I was on again. In one defense, the front chain attack, I was inside the attacker's circle so fast that they were in the air and landing in almost the same moment they started the swing. Someone in the crowd let out a low whistle.

Now I had only defending others and then armed gang attack. Don called out, "Armed gang attack: knife and club." I started slightly and blurted out, "You forgot defending others. That comes next."

Don didn't respond emotionally one way or the other. "Armed gang attack: knife and club. Begin now." I heard a rustle behind me and turned just in time to avoid a knife stab. Then I ducked under the club and took him down with a reverse hip throw that made his body into a shield. The knife flashed at me again and I got hold of his wrist and in one move forced his arm into his throat.

Puzzled and confused, I turned to look at Don and Jane, but they didn't smile. "Knife, club, and chain now." Something was going wrong. They weren't smiling and they were forcing this in a way different than I had set it up. My anger was rising. I didn't have time to give into it right then, because they were already moving toward me. I defended well again.

Just as I finished off the second group, a third one attacked. They had been told what to do before I had even finished. I got "killed" in this one. Then a fourth team was in. I took a knife cut on the arm at the last moment, but took him out as I took the cut.

"Defending others. Now." I turned fast, not sure of what was going on. There in front of me was Cheryl, one of the other students, walking down the mat away from me. She turned and looked at a male student standing by the edge of the mat. She stepped toward him and suddenly he reached out and grabbed her. She let out a scream and started backing up and trying to get away. I froze. This was the scenario from the street. She was screaming louder. I looked around at the table to check out what was happening ... they weren't at the table. I couldn't believe it. This wasn't fair. Those bastards! What right did they have to do this to me? And on my test. What were they thinking? I was almost panicked.

Between confusion, memories, and being betrayed I was raging. Don was behind me and Jane had moved off to one side of the man and the struggling woman. Don's eyes were burning into me. "Move, Les. Now. Do it." I was still frozen. "Do it now, or you will live with this regret the rest of your life."

I turned to the scene and started toward it thinking, "All right. If that's the way it is, I'll do it. Damn you, I'll do it, but if someone gets hurt, it's on your head." I was moving fast and was headed toward the male student when another stepped out and pulled a rifle from behind his back. He was now behind me. I was furious. And then I saw a fourth person in the scene. Only there was no body. Just a head, floating above us, a monstrous head ... My head. And I knew I was looking at my guardian. Oh, my God! I was getting ready to become my own version of the monster. My anger was driving me to hurt innocent students.

I kept moving, but I felt the anger slip away and I grabbed the first guy just as I had on the street. I pulled the blow an inch from his throat and turned to handle the other. There was no door and the rifle was coming up so I did a stepping kick backward and knocked the rifle away and took him out with a kick and a blow.

The male students had "fallen" and the victim was safe. I spun around expecting another sneak attack like the weapons attacks. There was no movement. I caught Jane's eyes. She smiled and softly said, "Congratulations. You passed."

I looked back at Don. He was smiling. I found myself half stating and half asking, "You did this to see if I would hurt someone if something similar happened. You wanted to know if my anger at the first two would drive me to hurt someone else."

"No," he said. "We wanted you to know who you really are and that you wouldn't hurt anyone without reason. You weren't sure if your monster was really your guardian. Now you know: He is. He warned you. And you—you are a Warrior-Priest. We have always known it. Now you do, too."

Suddenly, I was very tired. I dropped to my knees on the mats, my head on my chest. I barely noticed the applause. I did notice Jenna's touch as she wrapped her arms around me.

I was now a Black Belt. I had not realized it, but I had been hoping that in passing the test my pain would be over and my life would suddenly make sense. It didn't happen. True, I was relieved to have passed. True, I had learned and healed. But there was no miraculous cure, just another step toward healing. I was happy, thrilled, and a little disappointed that I hadn't gotten what I had secretly hoped for. But this had to be enough. And I know now that it was.

twenty

Ceremonies

It was the same kind of clear day that had begun this adventure for me just over two years ago, only now there was the crispness of the cold added to the mix. The caterers had been at work all morning, setting up tables and chairs around the walls. The Dojo had the mats in the middle as usual, and the altar had a white cloth draped over it. Jenna's sisters had draped white crepe paper all around the walls.

We had struggled over how to do the two ceremonies. Should we do two on one day, combine them, or do them on consecutive weekends? There was one part of us that wanted to be married in our gis, but at the same time Jenna had always seen her wedding as a little more traditional, which included a dress.

My parents represented the split of my families. My mother thought that a martial arts ceremony would be inappropriate for a wedding day; my father's side kept with the military history and saw them as a great combination. That didn't help Jenna and me at all.

A couple of weekends before we had visited her parents, and they were no help in the decision, either. We were sitting in the living room. Carol said that she would support us either way and thought that both would be very nice.

Luis' eyes were twinkling and he stated that whatever he said would probably turn out to be wrong and almost certainly would be considered insensitive. And that the last thing that he wanted to do was piss off a daughter with a Black Belt about her wedding day.

Jenna laughed and told him he was useless. He said, "Yes. I've heard that before and I've learned there is little point in arguing with a woman who has made up her mind."

"No, Dad. I haven't. That's the problem. I want your advice."

He looked over at me. "Don't let them draw you in with that ploy. She's just like her mother. They really have made up their mind when they say that. They just can't come out and say it. They have to hear you say something first and then they realize that that can't possibly be right and they are able to make up their mind for the opposite."

"Dad! I'm wanting some help here."

"And I'm wanting to survive this chapter of your life. Talk to your mother. I'm a cat with only a few lives left, and I don't want to lose another one over you getting married." With that he smiled, went over and kissed her on the cheek, and started out into the kitchen.

"Beer, Les?"

He and I beat a hasty retreat to the sound of a clucking chicken noise from Jenna. The women went on talking and laughing while her father and I got something to drink from the fridge and went on into the den.

The final conclusion was for a Black Belt ceremony with both of us in gis. After some photos, we would change into tux and dress, details to be worked out later. Mats would be folded up and then we would do the wedding.

Now the day had come. Don and Jane had offered the use of their house for changing purposes. The guests could wear whatever they chose to both ceremonies. Most of the club would probably wear gis to both. Those in the wedding party would change. Both sets of parents decided to wear their dress clothes to both ceremonies. food was going to be brought up at the last minute by the caterer and set out while we were taking pictures after the wedding.

I had worn my gi up, but had gotten there early so I could set out my tux and stuff in the house. Jenna did the same. We all met over at the Dojo and just before 10:00 Don and Jane came in, wearing their black gis and hakamas and with their swords belted to their sides.

The bowl sounded quietly, and I moved to the center front. The others lined up by rank and knelt on the mat. Guests seated themselves along the wall. Jenna had been told to sit to my right and just behind me. This was the first time I had seen this at a ceremony, but Don and Jane felt it was appropriate, given the day.

"Warriors stand on the boundary line. Sometimes metaphorically. Sometimes legally or politically. And sometimes they physically stand on the line between the victim and the oppressor.

"You know this. You have lived this. You have struggled with this. You know that this is not a game. It is for real. You moved into the drama and took your place. You stepped onto that line. You stood on the boundary line and this time you had to kill. You did not desire to kill, but it had to be done.

"This may have been the last time you will have to fight. It may not be the last. None of us know. We can only be there for those who need us and do what must be done.

"You were left behind. Warriors know. Warriors, the ones who were called, who were created to do battle, are condemned and blessed to a life of doing battle for the oppressed. For Warriors, the only real winner in battle is the Warrior who has 'crossed over the river and is resting in the shade of the tree.' It's sad to be left behind again, to know there are still more battles to fight. Look into the eyes of old Warriors and you will see it. In some ways the lucky ones are those who have gone on. They alone can rest now from a life of battles they never wanted in the first place.

"You were left behind. You are here and your family is glad. Your fiancée is glad. The world is rejoicing. An innocent person is safe and you are, too. It was a good day to die, but it was an even better day to have lived. We're glad you are still here. You have lived well."

I started as Jenna leaned forward and squeezed my forearm. I heard the sound of a sniffle, and glancing back, saw that there were tears in her eyes. Jane and Don were smiling and there was a pause in the rhythm of the speech. In that moment I heard Leroy start to clap and then the whole Dojo filled with the sound of the applause. Now the tears were forming in my eyes. When the sound died down, Don continued.

"You have struggled since that moment—struggled hard. Partly because you are a caring person and partly because of your personal history. Through your struggles you have become whole.

"Priests are persons called to heal. Some do so with the ritual of religions. Some heal through their hands or their teachings. But while they may occasionally be called to upon to fight, it is not of their nature more than it is for any other persons. More importantly, it is not of their calling.

"There is one sense in which all people should know how to be a warrior—with a little 'w'. If more people knew how to defend, then they would be less likely to be victims or to be bullies. But this is not the same as those who are called to be Warriors—large 'W'.

"Warriors are called to stand on the boundaries between victims and their oppressors. They are people of considerable skill. What is most impressive, however, is their ability to be the calm in the midst of the storm. They accept who they are and what their role is. Often a victim may be healed because of the protection of the Warrior, but the basic function of the Warrior is to defend, to protect."

Jane picked up and I turned my eyes toward her. "Warrior-Priests are those who live with one foot in each camp. They know of their calling to the higher values that they strive for, but all the while they also accept the realities and limitations of the world. Warrior-Priests often face the most internal stressors. Maintaining the balance between healing and protecting is hard.

"In the Western world this is especially hard, because we see these as opposites. In the Eastern world, the concept of polar opposites does not exist so much. They have other struggles. You are a Warrior-Priest."

And at that moment I saw even more clearly what they had been teaching me all along. This place had called me to itself to teach me what I needed to learn so that I could save another and stay alive myself. I saw myself more clearly now as I really had been those many months ago on the street, and even more of the pain slipped away.

Don took a deep breath and then continued. "You have accepted the calling of Warrior-Priest that was laid out for you when God laid the cornerstones of the universe. It was no accident that you were born in the time that you were, in the place that you were, in the family that you were. You came here at this time, this place for a purpose.

"You were not stamped out of a mold in some mass production line of souls. You were created as someone special. You were created for a special purpose. Before you were born, God knew your name, your *shem*, your power. God knew your name before your parents were born, or their parents, or their parent's parents. Your name was written in the

Book of Warriors before time began. You have now arrived to take your place among us."

His wife picked up the thread. "When you were led here, you were both blessed and cursed: blessed because you found the path to yourself, your calling, and your power; and cursed, because you now join the ranks of those called to change the world. You were not called to be the Messiah of the World, but you are called to be a messiah to your part of it.

"Today you receive your Black Belt. It is not being given to you. It is being awarded to you because you earned it. You earned it in class; you lived it on the street. You saw something in it before you even understood what that was, and you knew when you saw it that it was yours for the claiming. So you chose a path that had already been trodden by generations of Warriors gone before. You began the quest, you faltered, you exalted, you were bored, you were discouraged, you cried, you laughed, and most of all, you hung in when you didn't think you could go any farther. You did that during your test. You did that before your test.

"You lived through hell in the Pit. You came out the other side to face yourself on the street. In the midst of your struggle you were faced with an awful choice. You gave up your search for peace in order to save another. You chose well. But still you had to live through Hell on earth.

"In the midst of this struggle you found the seeds of your faith. You found your courage. Faith appears while you are waiting for hope to come. Courage is the act of moving ahead based on that faith. You did that well."

At that moment I thought to myself that the Black Belt I was to receive paled in comparison to what she had just said to me, but I know now that the meaning of the Black Belt is a symbol of the internal change in a person, not that the person had accomplished a set of skills. My Black Belt and what she had said were the same thing. Each person earns the belt in his or her own way, fighting his or her own internal battles.

"Make no mistake: courage is not a thing to be possessed. It is earned in moving beyond that which is hopeless, but must be done anyway. Courage is moving on when everyone else around you can no longer do anything but sit in the hopelessness of those who have given up.

"This Black Belt we now present you is not simply a reward, nor is it to be seen as just a point of pride. It is also an acceptance and reminder of your own death. By putting it on, you are accepting the responsibility of this process that you started before you understood who you really were. In accepting it, you are accepting that at any moment, you may be called upon to give up your life for that of someone else.

"This is your Black Belt. It is now time to remove the old belt and place the new one around you."

I stood and took my old Purple Belt off and placed the Black Belt around my waist. Don and Jane came up and asked me to kneel. I was caught off-guard, but did so. Jane motioned Jenna up beside me and they placed her hand in mine as she knelt beside me.

They placed their hands on our heads and there was absolute silence in the Dojo. They stood perfectly still and each leaned, one after the other, and whispered in my ear. In all the years since I have told only Jenna what they said. In my most recent years I have begun to write my funeral service, even though it should be a long time from now, according to stats. Still, I am well over halfway through my journey here in this world, and I know it is time to write it. On that day when I am buried with my belt, others will hear what words were given to me that day.

They held our hands and we stood up. Don and Jane hugged us and then Jenna hugged me. I turned to look at the class and the applause began. There was no cheering like the other ceremonies, but a quiet clapping that grew louder and kept going. Tears ran down my face. This place had been my source of power during the journey. And today the class had blessed me with this applause.

After a few minutes of pictures with different people, Don and Jane announced that it was time for us to change. They led us and several of the wedding party to their house, while others hung around at the Dojo.

I almost wished that I had done this on two different days so I could fully live in this moment. But at that moment we parted into different rooms to change and as I saw Jenna walk off in her gi, knowing that she was going to change into her dress for the wedding, I was overcome with emotion and knew that this had been right after all.

THE WEDDING

We had chosen a traditional wedding service in spite of the fact that all of our friends had written their own services. Once we had all changed we walked over as a group and met the others of the wedding party. We did not seat guests, but let them find their own seating during the interim. The remainder of the class had been asked to set up chairs, and by the time we got there everyone was seated.

As planned, Leroy and I went down front and stood to one side of the altar that had been pulled forward from the wall. The other grooms-men and bridesmaids lined up on either side of us. There was the sound of the prayer bowl from the back.

At that moment Don and Jane came through the doors in the back. They had asked if we wanted them to wear the traditional priestly robes of the church or the priestly garb of Waboku Jujitsu. We had opted for the latter even though we weren't sure what it was.

I looked up and was stunned. It was perfect for us. They came in slowly side by side. Their bleached white gis and hakamas were starched, and they each wore a pure scarlet belt around their waist.

Behind them came the bridesmaids, followed by my parents and siblings. Jenna's family came next. Don and Jane took their place in front of the altar. Once all of the families had been seated, Jane turned and gently rubbed the soft striker on the gong in a circle. Slowly the sound began to reverberate through the Dojo. Then the overtones took over, the room filled with sound, and my soul soared. As the sound began to fade, Jenna was escorted down the aisle by her father. She took her place by me.

"Dearly Beloved …"

And then it was over. I had kissed my bride and she kissed me back so enthusiastically that laughter rippled through the room. We turned and were introduced as a couple for the first time. In keeping with our desire for equality and in honor of Jenna's Hispanic background, we took a hyphenated last name.

We proceeded out the back of the Dojo to the haunting sound of the bowl and we were married. There was the usual confusion during pictures, lots of people hanging around, and finally the food and the feasting. The place eventually began to clear, and I looked around at the Dojo as if seeing it for the first time. I had found home here, I found myself here, and I found my wife here. And now these two ceremonies, both of beginnings, had come to an end on one day.

And they ended where I had begun the search into my soul just barely two years ago. Here, among the mats, the weapons, and the bags, with light streaming in the windows and the skylights, I stood by my bride. Here, where I found life in learning about the taking and protecting of life, I had come to open a new chapter. I stood, taking it all in, knowing that I was ready. Ready to start a new family.

Rising up in me was an overwhelming joy in my love of Jenna, a joy that had begun as fascination and hope on that first Sunday when I found my way to the Dojo. I was standing on the same spot as on that day, but I was no longer innocent and naive. I had experienced joy and terror, fear and anguish. I knew deeply what the poster on the wall meant.

"WABOKU JUJITSU – What to Do while Waiting for Peace to Come"

A wave of sadness swept over me for that short moment in time where death and life had come together in one place. I no longer believed that coming here had caused that terrible scene, just that my learnings here had allowed me to move through it, doing well what had to be done. Jenna said that she believed that my coming here had not caused it either, but rather that it had led me to that place and time, so that life and death could be more fairly played out for someone else.

I don't know if I could go that far. But, whether there was a cause-and-effect relationship, or simply circumstance, I had accepted what had happened and was slowly turning loose of the pain. Perhaps that was all I could do at that point in my journey. Without this place I wouldn't have met her. Without this place I might not have lived through that moment. Without this place I might not have lived long enough to be here beside her today.

I looked at Jenna, then at her family, and then at mine. I felt reality slipping again, and this time I relaxed into it. I came to, in another phase of being. I was still here in the Dojo, standing next to Jenna, but we were middle-aged, and Don and Jane were old. Then, almost immediately, that vision also began to slip away. I came to, back in the day I had started in, and I was standing there in the Dojo next to my bride, surrounded by family and friends and overwhelmed with a sense of joy and contentment.

I had a deep sense of joy in the moment and contentment with life as a whole. I could not see what events, what joys, and what tragedies were yet to come, but I knew whom I would face them with and that together we would work, side by side, to find openings where there were none.

And that was enough.

New Years Day, 2010

Dear Ted,

Wow … two years ago your questions prompted me to write *Sundays in the Dojo*, and now here you are and ready to test for your first belt degree.

It seems so strange and yet so natural to have you in class in the Dojo. Strange, because for years you were "just" a family member who wandered in and out of the Dojo; natural because we've always felt that you were always headed this way.

And you are good at this art. I know that you feel awkward sometimes, but in truth, you are a natural. You remind me of myself when I began. I've watched you, and often you seem to be remembering more than learning something new.

As the New Year approached, I found myself wanting to write to you on the second anniversary of the first letter. In that, there was one question that I said I would answer later, when the time was right. You asked about the Warrior in our family that you and your sister were named after.

It's now time to tell you about her. Her name was Theodora Helena Etherby, a female warrior in a time and culture when females weren't considered to even be able to fight. She died in a small village in England the early months of 1907.

We know little of her except for what she chose to leave behind in one short letter. What we do know is enough to show how remarkable a woman—person—she was. She was a Warrior.

During your growing up years your grandmother or I would sometimes quote something from "The Warrior's Codex" to you or Helena.

This is a collection of sayings that this woman gathered together from all over the world during her lifetime of travels. It is well over a hundred years old now, and parts of it may be over a hundred-fifty years old.

The Codex itself is showing signs of age and heavy use. We need to protect it, so we have had it scanned and had electronic and hard copies of it made. We are also talking with a librarian at the university near here about how to preserve the actual Codex.

Don and Jane started a tradition that it would only be shown to those who have reached Black Belt in our system. You will also get to see it once you have attained this rank. I was the one exception, due to the circumstances you already know.

For reasons that I won't go into right now, we have decided to publish the Codex for the public. We think that it is time; kairos and chronos have come together. So what of the tradition of only allowing Black Belts to see it? Well, we will continue that by only allowing Black Belts to see and read from the original.

The most important question for you now, however, is how Theodora Helena Etherby relates to us as family. I told you in that first letter that there are many ways to be family. She was not family by bloodline. While bloodline is important, marriage and birth are not the only ways to become family. Sometimes family lines are based on a spiritual heritage that can tie us together even more tightly than genetics.

Ted, we are all created special and are put here in this world in this, our time in history, to fulfill our appointed tasks and to leave the world a better place than we found it. T. H. Etherby found her purpose in life by becoming a Warrior in spite of her gender and the age and culture in which she lived. We know she fought at least once with deadly efficiency, but we do not have any other details. What we do know is that she collected sayings of the heart and soul of a Warrior and put them together into the Warrior's Codex.

How Jane and Don came into possession of it, I don't know. When we took over the Dojo during their last years, they only said it came to them as a responsibility and that they were now passing it on to us. Jane and Don are also part of our spiritual family, and we are continuing their line and legacy. Someday, we will pass it on to the next generation of Warrior-Priests.

Perhaps it will be you, and/or Helen, or perhaps by then you will have found that your path to power lies elsewhere. Whatever is right for you will become clear in time, and that is as it should be.

Until that time you need to study here for as long as it seems right. We will support you in any decision you make: stay or go—it doesn't matter. What matters is that you find your own power and that you live out your life well.

We love you, and it is a rare privilege to have you in our class in the Dojo.

Love,

Grandpa Les

22nd Century Institute

**Passing on the Mantle of Personal
Power – Generation to Generation**
Founders/Directors: Revs. Don and Jane Lewis, Ph.D.s
We are Experts in Spiritual/Personal Formation:
We Teach Leaders How to Train Leaders.

The measure of any generation is not how well their children do, but how well their children raise their children. Thus, the name of the Institute. We must look at least two generations ahead when working to become the best version of ourselves.

We have raised two children into a successful adulthood, fought and both won and lost some of life's battles, and lived through moments of sheer terror and extreme joy. We have lived fully during periods of extreme stress and periods of deep peace. In short, we have always chosen to live life fully regardless of what has been thrown at us.

During our lives we have run a wilderness camp and mountaineering school, a mountain rescue team, ridden with rescue squads, taught in public schools, community colleges to graduate schools, spent over twenty years as executives doing turn-arounds in conference centers, worked in the public mental health field and had a sex therapy and spirituality private practice. During these times we created Waboku Jujitsu and hold Warrior-Priest degrees in the that art./

Our underlying work in all of these fields was to use the setting we were in to help people become the best version of themselves. We found leaders and trained them to excel in their life and their chosen field.

If the opportunity should arise we would love to meet you and to work with you as fellow travelers to become all that we were created to be.

22nd Century Institute

**Passing on the Mantle of Personal
Power – Generation to Generation**

Services

Speaking, Teaching and Training

We will work with you to develop up to date, organizationally relevant presentations ranging from keynote speeches to multi-day training seminars. Contact us at directors@22ci.org for more information or details.

We train workers in government agencies in the theoretical and practical aspects of mental health issues and de-escalation techniques. We also train police officers in these topics for Crisis Intervention Team training (a 40 hour DOJ approved course of study) We also can provide similar training for churches and judicatories.

Martial Arts:

We are especially interested in training Sensei in teaching the soft skills needed to train their students in personal growth and formation, ethics, and finding the path to their personal power.

Counselors/Therapists/Coaches/Pastors:

We lead state, regional, and national level conference trainings in the areas of spirituality, sexuality, and growing themselves and their clients along the paths to personal power.

Excerpts from

The Warrior's Codex

"Courage is not living without fear. It is living in spite of fear. It is doing what must be done despite your panic.
Courage requires trusting both yourself and God.
And that is truly living."

* * *

"When you find that your enemy is yourself, the only path to success is through your fear.
Find what is making you afraid and go straight into it."

* * *

"Fear is a great servant but a terrible master."

* * *

"The Warrior's Blessing
Go now in peace,
But if someone should keep you from being able to do that —
May you live the next few moments well.

www.ingramcontent.com/pod-product-compliance
Lightning Source LLC
Chambersburg PA
CBHW030525020726
47494CB00004B/1240

OTHER BOOKS BY THE AUTHOR

The Warrior's Codex: Sayings from the Heart of a Warrior

UPCOMING BOOKS by Revs. Don and Jane Lewis, Ph.D.s

Beyond Technique in the Dojo: The Making of a 22nd Century Warrior

Winning the Sex, God, and Religion Battles: Therapeutic Interventions, Pastoral Care, and Personal Growth

CONTACT INFORMATION

For bulk book orders, seminar information, and coaching:

directors@22ci.org

Websites:
www.22ci.org

Don S. and Jane H. Lewis
PO Box 356
Stanardsville, VA 22973